Praise for Bigfoot Mountain

A beautiful and engrossing tale of a mighty child, a magnificent forest and the mysteries which bind us all in the best ways – this is a rich and powerful book, a real triumph of love, wisdom and storytelling.

Horatio Clare

Bigfoot Mountain transports readers into the heart of the forest and allows them to see the wild from the perspective of the beings who know it best. A skilful interweaving of modern family relationships and wilderness adventure.

Nicola Davies

An innovative and moving story, filled with wonderful descriptions of the West Coast wilderness.

Tyler Keevil

A compelling story of courage, protecting nature and finding your way.

Erin Hamilton

Roderick O'Grady

BIGFOOT ISLAND

Harris!

I hope you
enjoy!

Rod

BIGFOOT
ISLAND

RODERICK O'GRADY

Firefly

First published in 2023 by Firefly Press
25 Gabalfa Road, Llandaff North, Cardiff, CF14 2JJ
www.fireflypress.co.uk

A CIP catalogue record of this book is available
from the British Library.

1 3 5 7 9 8 6 4 2

ISBN 978-1-915444-09-7
ebook ISBN 978-1-915444-10-3

This book has been published with the support of
the Books Council of Wales.

Typeset by Elaine Sharples
Cover and internal illustration by Jess Mason:
www.jessmasonillustration.com

Printed and bound by CPI Group (UK) Ltd, Croydon, Surrey, CR0 4YY

To my children Oona and Gus, who scampered
with me through the forest

BIGFOOT MOUNTAIN

MINNIE

Chapter One

With her feet together, both Minnie's trainers nearly fitted inside the footprint.

The indentations left by the Bigfoot had been stepped on so many times by the small pointed hooves of passing deer that it was barely discernible. Pine needles had filled the dips and dents in the mud, and rain had dripped on the footprints, softening the edges. Minnie lifted a small pine branch that had dropped from above or been knocked off by a passing creature. Using it as a brush, she swept away the leaf litter to reveal a second huge footprint.

Next to her, in a patch of brilliant sunshine, Musto stretched out his shaggy yellow front legs and settled onto his side, his back against a stand of ferns. He wagged his tail on the earth of the game trail. Minnie bent to ruffle his neck fur and

1

to stroke his head, fondling his floppy ears, then stood and stepped the longest step her legs would allow her. It reached nowhere close to the third footprint. Further along the trail, in the fourth print, she noticed where the little toe had been splayed out slightly when the foot had slipped on the earth. It had been dry when she and Billy had found the footprints a few weeks ago, and the trail was well used by deer and other forest creatures so the ground had been quite bare, exposing the soil beneath the grass and ferns. It had been so unusually dry at that time that there had been fires on the mountain ranges in the east – terrible fires that had ravaged many miles of tinder-dry forest. Now the ground was damp as the usual summer rains had returned. Trees dripped and tiny jewels of moisture clung to silk strands slung across the trail by busy spiders.

Minnie surveyed the forest carefully, peering up the trail at the dark spaces between the cedar trees, the firs, pines and scrubby bushes. Birds were singing, whistling and peeping; bugs were humming. Wind swayed strands of pale lichen from low limbs and shifted the higher branches, rattling them gently above her. Serenity, and a sense of connection to the land, the trees, and all the roaming creatures who made the mountain slopes their home, came welling up, and she filled her lungs, flung wide her arms and yelled as loudly as she could, '*Hellooo…!*'

She wasn't really expecting a reply but she did strain her ears in case, somewhere on the upper slopes, the maker of the footprints had heard her, taken up a stout stick and swung it hard against a tree trunk. But there was no answering knock, no long whooping call.

Turning to retreat down the game trail, something caught her eye. Beyond the fourth footprint, where the trail rose slightly before dipping through a ferny hollow, was a small pile of pinecones.

'What's this?'

Musto padded to her side. Three pinecones had been placed close together with a fourth sitting on top. Musto sniffed them, took a step back and looked up into the forest. The rich deep-brown scales were closed tight, and as Minnie lifted the top cone it felt damp to the touch. She gazed at it like she'd never seen a pinecone before.

Smiling, she pressed her freckly nose to it.

'Hmm ... piney.' She looked up into the shadows of the forest. 'Thank you!'

The young girl and the yellow dog ran back down the trail through the spruce, pines and cottonwood trees.

Minnie sat high up in her favourite pine tree, hugging the slender trunk as it swayed gently in the summer breeze. From her lofty perch she had a fine view of the surrounding land and sea: their five small cabins on the grassy slope down to the bay, each with a perfect view of the water, today flat and calm like stretched grey silk; the small tree-tufted inshore islands; and the larger island lying across the bay like a reclining giant under an emerald-green blanket.

Directly below her tree, on one side, was the fenced-in square of vegetable garden, close to the eight tall foundation posts on which their old cabin used to sit – the cabin they'd demolished so the mountain's Bigfoot clan could use their ancient route to the sea. On the other side of her tree was the dusty space where her stepfather,

Dan, and their neighbour, Connie, parked their trucks. If she twisted on her branch Minnie could see the track she'd just walked down, past Connie's cabin, the deck adorned in garlands of white honeysuckle, where Connie lived with Billy, who was a couple of years younger than Minnie, and Musto the dog. Behind their cabin stretched the steep forested slopes and deep, dark ravines of Bigfoot Mountain.

Minnie and Dan were living in one of the smaller cabins while he built them a new and improved home. Their new cabin's first level, set on stout posts, was nearly complete, with a wide deck wrapping round it on three sides. It was to be bigger than the old cabin, and positioned close to the rocky outcrop on which sat the black solar panels and the spinning white wind turbine.

Bags of tools and coils of power cables sat on plywood panels that were neatly stacked on the grass. Dan was re-using the lumber from the deconstructed cabin, but there had been a delivery this morning from town, and Minnie could see him carrying pale brown planks of freshly sawn wood up the steps to the deck.

Minnie's curly brown hair was tied back in an

optimistic attempt to prevent it snagging on twigs as she climbed. Multiple coils of her hair were hooked on bits of rough bark or hanging in tendrils from twigs. She'd climb up the tree at least once a day. It was her special place to sit, remember her mom, and just *be*.

As she sat on her perch, a foot securely tucked under a lower branch, something caught her eye near the big island on the far side of the bay – something that hadn't been there yesterday.

A bee buzzed around her head, hovered by her yellow T-shirt and landed on her white shorts. She ignored it, fully engrossed in what she could see emerging from the haze where the large green island's stretch of shore met the sea. Lifting her binoculars to her freckled face and squinting, she peered at the tiny white object glinting in the low morning sunshine.

Known locally as Echo Island and thought to be uninhabited, Minnie knew that it *was* in fact inhabited, but not by humans.

Minnie now thought of it as Bigfoot Island.

The water of the bay that separated the coastline from Bigfoot Island was slightly choppy on the far side and the grey water was sprinkled with white plumes. On Minnie's short stretch of shoreline at Cabin Cove the surface was calmer, the incoming breeze buffered by the pines, the stunted sea-oaks and the spiky broom bushes on the cluster of small outlying islands.

'What do we have here, bee?' she murmured.

The bee buzzed off towards the mountain, perhaps to feed at Connie's blooming honeysuckle.

'Oh, no. No, no. Not good.'

Minnie lowered the binoculars and looked down.

'Hey!' she yelled. 'Dad!'

Dan looked up from where he was working on the cabin deck.

'Look!' Minnie pointed out across the water. Dan shielded his eyes from the sun and peered at the white boat heading towards them.

It took a few minutes for Minnie to climb down her tree and, sprinting across the mown grass, she joined him, breathless, on the deck of their temporary home.

Dan was looking through his 'binos' at the advancing boat.

'Recognise it?'

'No, I don't.'

It had been two weeks since they had stood on this deck and watched in stunned silence as an entire clan of ten Bigfoots had sneaked through the property from tree to tree, bush to bush, shadow to shadow, before running and jumping from the end of the jetty, plunging into the icy cold sea and swimming westward towards Bigfoot Island. It was an event that was so earth-shatteringly unusual that it had profoundly affected all four humans who had witnessed it. The effect it had had on the intrepid Musto was an enduring mystery.

Fishing boats would pass by out in the bay most days and their lights could be seen at night, but now a large boat they did not know was heading straight towards them from the island, and it was not a fishing boat.

'Small passenger vessel ... custom pilothouse ... hard to see at this angle, straight on. Maybe as much as forty or fifty footer! Nice!'

Minnie jabbed Dan in the ribs gently with her elbow. 'It's not nice, it's awful! We do not need a boatload of tourists cluttering up the place.'

'Yes, we do. Maybe they'll want to stay a few nights.'

'Then they should have booked online, like everyone else.'

'There is nobody else, Min. We need the business. Coastal Fire Centre gave us the all-clear days ago, you know that. We're open.'

The smoke clouds from the enormous weeks-long wildfires, the result of a freakishly hot summer, were gone at last. As she stared at the distant mountain top, crowned with a flat ridge of dark green, she whispered softly, 'Stay up there. Stay up there.'

Minnie trotted down the steps. 'I'm going to consult Billy.'

She headed back up the slope towards the track. Stopping near the half-built new cabin, she glanced back at the white boat still less than halfway across the sound. Holding out a straight arm with her thumb up, she squinted and estimated the boat size was still less than the size of her thumbnail.

'Reckon about … twenty minutes.'

She walked by the fenced-in vegetable garden in which she had spent pretty much all of the last two weeks digging, weeding and tidying. Working alone there had helped the events of that momentous night to settle, though the images were still vivid and played often in her mind.

She could easily recall the massive black head of the young Bigfoot rising up from below the far end of the deck, next to the seemingly lifeless body of a crow they'd just noticed there, lying on its back. When the Bigfoot had placed a huge hand gently over the bird, it had stirred, kicking its spindly black legs, flapped its wings, and flown away. The amazement and wonder that she, Dan, Connie and Billy had experienced was overwhelming, but had been accompanied by a strange and profound sense of calm.

She hurried through the flattened patch of bare earth where the eight posts stuck out of the ground, each much taller than Minnie, and up the grassy track. Connie and Billy were Minnie's only neighbours for many miles, so if she wanted a chat, they were the only option. Connie's cabin, close to the forest, was easily the prettiest – the wooden rail of the long, wide deck smothered in twisting green climbers, the sweet aroma from white flowers attracting a constant humming mass of butterflies, wasps, moths and, of course, bees.

Minnie smiled at the busy insects. 'Oh hi, bees and wasps and butterflies, and … hey, Billy! Billy-Bug!'

First out of the screen door was Musto, grinning goofily, swiping his shaggy yellow tail with delight as he bounded over to Minnie, who stood on the top step, one hand resting on a deck post and the other on her hip. The dog tossed his head begging for a caress. She knelt and fussed over him.

Connie emerged from the cabin with a green apple in her hand. 'Hi Minnie.'

She wore a long, loose dress with a scattering of small blue flowers across it and her feet were bare. Her thick black hair with its one streak of grey was pulled back off her face and tied with a turquoise-coloured beaded band.

'Hi Connie.'

Billy burst from the cabin, all shaggy blond hair, long, skinny arms, baggy shorts and bare feet.

Minnie stood up, one hand on the post the other on her hip.

'Hey Bill.'

'Hey.'

'Yeah, hi.'

'Yeah, hi.'

11

'What's up, Billy?'

'Not much. Why are you standing like that?'

'This is how brave adventurers stand when they have important news to share.'

'What news?' asked Billy.

'The Bigfoots are coming back.'

'Wait! What? Where? Whaddya mean?'

Connie pointed down the slope. 'What's Dan doing?'

Dan was still on the deck of the cabin peering through his binoculars. From this higher vantage point there was a clear view of the cabins and beyond them the small islands, the wide empty mass of seawater and, ploughing across towards them, the white boat.

'Dan is looking at the boat the Bigfoots are on.'

Connie and Billy were used to Minnie's particular brand of humour, but Billy rated his friend as super-smart, as brave as a lion, and someone around whom interesting things happened. So he looked closely at Minnie, who kept a straight face, until she cracked, announcing, 'Ha! Gotcha Billy-Boy!'

'You did not get me: Bigfoots on a boat!'

Connie shaded her eyes. 'That's not a fishing boat.'

'Yeah, bad news! We have visitors.'

'Want to go up in the forest, Billy-Bug? Musto could use another stretch of the old legs, huh, Musto?'

'No thanks.'

'The Bigfoots are gone, Billy. They're over on Bigfoot Island. We saw them go.'

'Yeah, I know. I remember it well.'

'Don't you want to see who's on that boat?' asked Connie taking a bite out of the apple. 'It's heading this-a-way.'

Minnie was looking up at the mountain. 'Not particularly.'

Connie crossed the deck to where Minnie knelt stroking Musto's head. She handed her the apple. 'Not ready to share this place, Min?'

Her thick black braid hung over her shoulder, and she tickled Minnie's nose with the end of it. Minnie grinned.

Connie stood up. 'Let's go check out this boatload of Bigfoots.'

Minnie moved to sit on the steps, munching on the apple. 'I'll catch up with you.'

She was hungry. Dan's lunch times were erratic, so she usually just helped herself when hunger pangs struck. She passed the apple to Billy who took a big bite, handed it back and launched himself off the steps, rolling on the grass on landing, and running down the path after his mother and Musto.

Minnie ate the apple to the core and, hurling it high into the trees across the track, announced, 'Free lunch, bugs!'

She stepped on to the trail and stood facing the forest. 'Do not come down here, mister! Nothing to see here!' Then she gazed into the distance at the advancing boat and at Dan, Connie and Billy walking down to meet it.

She had held on to her extraordinary secret for two weeks, since the night the Bigfoots left, and she wasn't sure how much longer she could keep it to herself.

Billy looked perplexed. 'Why doesn't it come in closer?'

Minnie, Dan, Connie and Billy stood on the floating jetty where their two small rowboats were moored, one painted blue, and one painted green.

The big white boat was resting at anchor out in the deeper water.

Dan raised the binoculars to his eyes.

'Tide will be turning soon, and it won't be deep enough for that vessel to moor up any closer.'

They watched its black inflatable dinghy being lifted off the roof of the cabins and winched out over the side to be lowered on to the water.

'How many people have you seen on board, Dan?'

'Not many, Connie.' He lowered his binos. 'Maybe four. Looks like a couple and their son and the skipper of the boat. That's it.'

The dinghy was pulled round to the stern of the boat, where a safety rail was swung open like a gate. Now the couple and a tall, slim boy stepped down off the platform at the back and sat in the inflatable. The older man with the rope stepped confidently into the dinghy and pushed off from the vessel. He pulled on the starter rope and the motor roared, spluttering in the water, briefly spewing a cloud of blue-grey smoke.

Dan turned to the others. 'OK, at the risk of stating the obvious, no one mentions the 'B' word. Got it?'

The smiling skipper lobbed a rope up onto the jetty. 'Permission to come ashore?'

Minnie grabbed it up and whipped it round a post, cinching it tight. She was watching the visitors closely and Connie placed a comforting hand on her shoulder.

'Sure. Welcome,' said Dan, as the slim teenager stepped ashore.

The skipper was holding the jetty side with his hand, as he stood bent over in the dinghy. 'I'm Sam Tooke. That's my boat out there, the *Squamish Queen*.'

Minnie noted his grey hair and beard and reckoned he was pretty old. He reached up and shook Connie's hand. On his right forearm was a tattoo of a stylized eagle head in profile.

'Hi Sam, I'm Dan. This is my neighbour, Connie, and our kids, Minnie and Billy.'

Sam looked bemused.

The other man stepped on to the jetty, 'Hi. Friendly neighbours, huh? I like this place already. I'm Alex.'

He was younger than Sam, but Minnie reckoned

he was older than Dan, because he had grey sideburns and the stubble on his chin was white, whereas Dan's beard was mostly still black.

'Oh, no, I mean, we're not...' Dan began. 'Connie is Billy's mom and I am Minnie's dad. They live in the cabin up the track. This is, well, these are our cabins: mine and Minnie's, Minnie's and mine. Minnie and I own these cabins.'

Minnie patted his arm. 'I think they've got it.'

'OK... Well, I'm Alex Ashton-Kitto, this is my wife Cristy, and that's our boy Marshal. Good to meet you.'

Minnie looked at the teenager. He had straight brown hair with a fringe that covered his eyes. He wore jeans and a long-sleeved shirt buttoned at the wrists, even though it was a hot day and everyone else except Connie was wearing shorts.

'Beautiful spot you have here,' said Alex.

'Stunning,' agreed Cristy.

Sam had climbed out of the dinghy and was tying a second rope to a post.

'Thanks,' said Dan.

Cristy admired the cabins, the pines, the grassy slope up to the forest. 'Just lovely,' she said.

And blessed shade from these pine trees. It's heavenly.'

She took off her wide-brimmed hat and long blonde locks cascaded to her shoulders.

'Nothing much happens here,' said Minnie, noticing the way the sun lit Cristy's hair so it seemed to gleam, like Musto's yellow fur after he'd been bathed. 'But the forest … well, the forest is crawling with dangerous animals – like bears, mountain lions, rabid moose…'

'Really?' asked Billy. 'I thought…'

'Minnie, please! Stop that.' Dan held her arm.

'Do not go into the forest!' Minnie said, twisting away from Dan.

'I'm sorry, she's…'

'Exaggerating,' said Connie.

'Slightly. Slightly exaggerating,' said Minnie.

Alex grinned broadly, 'Rabid moose! That's quite an imagination you have!'

'Musto!' called Billy.

The dog was sniffing about on the shore, typically busy, looking for crabs, sea slugs and worms.

Dan pulled off his cap and wiped his brow. 'It is perfectly safe here.'

'And very quiet,' said Connie. 'So peaceful.'

'Except...' Now, they all looked at Billy. 'Except for ... the fire.'

'Fire?' asked Cristy.

Billy pointed at the mountain. 'Forest fire. Massive, devastating forest fire.'

'Yes!' Minnie nodded at Billy. 'Devastating forest fire. In the forest!'

Dan waved a hand vaguely eastwards. 'Way over on the other side of the mountain. It's out now. Very much out.'

'Oh sure, yeah, we heard about that,' said Sam. 'Saw the smoke, for weeks.'

'So, this is your summer vacation trip?' asked Connie.

'Yeah, Sam's been taking us all over,' said Alex. 'Fishing, relaxing. I do photography. Cristy does not have my sea legs, it has to be said. She has great legs but not sea legs.' He laughed. No one else did. 'We'd love a few days ashore if you have any vacancies at all.'

'Do we ever!' said Dan. 'We've been closed due to the fire. Take your pick. We're in this cabin here, while we're re-building. But the others are empty.'

'Oh, wow, they're all so cute.' Cristy pointed at cabin number four up on the rise. 'How about that one up there?'

'Good choice,' said Minnie. 'The white one. Soon to be pink. We're re-painting them all soon.'

Dan looked at Minnie. 'Are we?'

Musto came bounding on to the deck. He sniffed everyone in turn, and received strokes and pats with glee.

Billy turned to the teenage boy. 'Hi Marshal. This is my dog, Musto. Are you good at math?'

Marshal gazed resolutely at his phone. 'Hi. No. Got wifi here?'

Cristy grasped the boy's wrist. 'Marshal! Please.'

'Sixteen year olds,' said Alex. 'What are ya gonna do?'

'Accidentally drop their phone in the sea?' Minnie suggested as she brushed past Marshal and marched up towards cabin number one.

'Minnie…' began Dan, but he let her go.

Standing inside the cabin, slightly back from the window, Minnie watched Dan and Connie lead the couple up the slope to cabin number four as Musto bounded on ahead with Billy. The boy, Marshal, still looking at his phone, was following slowly. He stopped to kick a stone. It didn't roll very far, and he picked it up and flung it at the sea. It bounced off a rock and plopped into the water just beyond the swash where the waves lapped at the narrow beach.

Minnie pulled a wooden chair out from the table and sat gazing out of the window. Sam, now back at the big white boat anchored out by the first small island, was retying the dinghy. Three white gulls sitting on the sky-blue roof of the pilothouse flapped and lifted away when Sam stepped aboard.

It was strange for Minnie to see a boat anchored out there. They rarely had visitors from the sea. Sometimes cabin renters took one of their two rowing boats to explore the islands and to fish for their supper, but there had been no renters since the forest fire had sparked into life many, many weeks ago.

Minnie thought of the times she and her mom would paddle a canoe along the shore and round the closest islands. They would catch fish from lines dangled casually from the canoe, sometimes a small salmon and sometimes sea trout, which was her favourite. They would grill them on the deck of the cabin, their old cabin, now demolished, the cabin where Minnie was born and where her mother had died.

A toppling blast of sadness hit her and she put her head on her folded arms; her shoulders shuddered as she wept. Waves of sorrow would sometimes sweep over the twelve-year-old and she'd feel she was drowning in grief and all she could do was go climb up her tree and wait for the wind to blow her tears dry.

There was a knock at the door. It opened slowly.

'Hello-dee-doo-daa,' said Billy. 'That's what the British say instead of hi.'

'Do they?' mumbled Minnie from her elbow.

'Yes, they do. You OK?'

Minnie nodded.

Backing out, Billy slowly pulled the door shut. 'In that case, cheerio!'

Chapter Two

Grabbing her water bottle and a small wicker basket, Minnie pushed open the cabin door, jumped down the steps and hurried up the slope to the vegetable garden. She could hear faint chatter from cabin number four but resolved not to look across at the 'guests' enjoying the peace and serenity of her home.

The tall gate, which was a simple wooden frame with chicken wire fastened across it, creaked open and swung shut with a gentle *klunk* behind her. The fence was high to keep out the deer, but not strongly built – it would collapse in a heap of wood and wire if a person tried to climb over. It occurred to Minnie that if the Bigfoots had wanted to eat the veg they could just have pushed the fence over. They hadn't done that. Minnie reckoned it was maybe because they respected the space her mom had worked in for so long. Or maybe they didn't know it was here, and the night they had ventured down they were perhaps too busy to notice it.

Minnie had worked in the garden every day since the Bigfoots left the forest and it was now tidy and largely weed-free. With Dan's help she'd replaced the wooden boards that edged each separate bed, and she'd stretched netting over the new kale seedlings, just sprouting now after she'd planted them a week ago. The slugs and snails would munch through any new green growth, so she had spread eggshells and dry seaweed around to deter them. Birds would eat what they could; she'd seen pigeons, seagulls, ravens, sparrows, yellow warblers, black-capped chickadees and tiny bushtits visiting the garden, so she'd strung up lengths of string from the top of the fence across to the opposite top of the fence and attached long strips of aluminium foil, which seemed to deter them.

Minnie knelt and pulled at the stem of a leafy plant and a cluster of small creamy-yellow potatoes emerged from the dark earth. Digging around with her fingers she searched for any loose spuds that had broken away from the network of tubers underground. A worm, dislodged from its earthy home, curled defensively into a knot. Between finger and thumb Minnie gently placed it on the loose soil and covered it over.

'Dig, Wormy. Dig your way to safety.'

'Permission to enter the garden?'

'Oh! You startled me, Connie.'

'Sorry.'

Connie crouched down nearby. Musto followed her through the gate and immediately began snuffling in the loose earth.

'Good boy Musto, dig 'em up.' Minnie stroked his shaggy golden coat. 'The spuds, Musto, not the worms!'

'They're OK, those folks.' Connie sat on the ground between the beds. 'He's trying too hard to impress, that Alex, but they're OK. They live in Los Angeles. So glamorous.'

Minnie lobbed a handful of spuds into her basket. 'He's older than Dan.'

'Yeah. So? Oh, right. She's much younger. She's maybe his second or even third wife.'

'Third? Wow.'

'It happens. Specially in LA. Sam's gone back to the boat to get their stuff. He's going to take us out on a little trip up the inlet some time.'

Minnie dropped another potato in the basket. 'How long are they staying?'

'They said three days. They want to go hiking.'

Minnie sharply turned her head to look across at Connie. 'In the forest? On the mountain?'

'Yes. Where else?'

Minnie rubbed soil off a good-size potato with her thumbs. Connie knelt to help, digging with her fingers.

'Connie, has anyone ever asked you to keep a secret?'

'Ah ha! Secrets! Of course… Not for a while though. Living out here there's not a lot of secrets to keep.'

'What was the last secret you were told?'

'Well, my friend Lulu Finch works at Roy's Beer 'n' Grill, and she told me…' She abruptly stopped working the soil and peered at Minnie.

'Minnie, are you trying to catch me out? I ain't tellin' ya!'

They laughed.

'You have failed my cunning test, Connie. I really don't think I can trust you with a secret!'

Connie stood up, still smiling wryly. 'OK well, you clearly need to share, so I'll go get Billy.'

'No!'

They laughed again.

'Dan?' asked Connie.

'No, I don't want him to worry.'

'Now I am really intrigued.'

Connie sat down on the patchy grass dividing the beds, as Minnie lifted a small wooden peg from the earth and handed it to her. It was carved flat on one side and handwritten in small, neat, black letters were the words, *Juliette Potatoes. Great roasted, mashed, boiled or baked – see recipe 13.'*

'Oh! Oh my! This is Georgina's writing!'

'Yes, I found Mom's recipes in the cabin. They have little messages for me written on them. It's like she knew I would eventually come in this garden and, you know, do some work, and find these pegs!'

'Is this your secret? It's wonderful. Dan would love this.'

'This isn't the secret, and he knows. I've been cooking her recipes.'

'What is it then, Minnie?'

Minnie turned her head away, looking up at the mountain. Connie's hazel brown eyes followed the young girl's gaze.

'The one that showed himself to us, that night…'

'Yes?'

'I saw him.'

'Yes, by the deck, we all saw him, Minnie. It was wonderful. Profoundly mind-blowing, and hugely unsettling, but … but wonderful.'

'I saw him walk back up to the forest.' She turned to look at Connie. 'He didn't follow them, the others. He's up there now. Alone. Don't tell Dan.'

Connie took Minnie's hand, and very softly asked, 'Is he watching us?'

Minnie leant in and whispered. 'Maybe. I can't tell. But I don't think so.'

Tears sprang to Connie's eyes, her body visibly shuddered and her face turned pale. She slowly turned to look up at the mass of forest that reached to the very edge of her property – at the trees and bushes and tall ferns that stood silent and still by the dusty track that led up to and past her home.

'He's the one who helped me when I fell in the forest and knocked myself out, and I woke up to find pine resin smeared on the cut on my head. Remember? I just know it. I know he's the one. I knew it when he looked at me that night on the deck. After all the others had jumped in to the sea.'

Sitting together on the grass between the potato patch and the tomatoes, they stared up at the forest, their eyes searching the shadows.

'It's OK, Connie, he's keeping us safe. But I'm worried.'

Connie searched Minnie's eyes. 'Worried?'

'Yes. I'm worried that he will be curious about these new people and come too close, and that more people will come and will hunt him, and scare him away, or … or worse…'

Connie stood up, dusting grass and twigs off her flowery blue dress, still looking up at the trees. 'OK. Well, I'm sure your friendly Sasquatch will be just fine … and will stay away… I'm going to … to fix me and Billy some … er, some food now.'

She dropped her sandals, shuffled her feet into them, and adjusted the elastic hairband at the end of her black braid.

'Do you want me to come with you, Connie?'

'No, no. Thanks.'

And Connie, followed by Musto, pushed open the garden gate, paused with a hand on the closest standing post, then walked up the track towards her cabin. Watching her go, Minnie wondered if perhaps it would have been kinder to tell Dan instead of Connie.

Minnie stood where the grassy slope meets the shore, watching Dan collecting beached timber. This driftwood had been in the water a long time and, having been buffeted by rocks along the shore and baked by the sun and buffeted some more, the bark had been worn off, and the wood was a gleaming smooth silver-grey.

'What ya gonna do with that?'

'Well, some we could use for the deck rail, the thin ones, or for supports, you know, to support the banister rail.'

'The what?'

'The banister. The thing you hold on to when climbing stairs.'

'Oh. Right. Nice. Need a hand, Dan?'

'Er, no, thanks. I've got it.'

'In that case, do you need a *handstand*, Dan?' She kicked up into a handstand, tottered as her arms collapsed, and tumbled on to the grass. Dan laughed. Minnie laughed too, as she got to her feet and sat on a nearby boulder. Sam was pottering about on the white boat. They could see him pushing a bucket across the deck as he mopped.

'What does *Squamish Queen* mean?'

Dan looked out at the white vessel. 'Squamish is a district down the coast a-ways.'

'Oh, yeah. Right.' Minnie twisted round to look up at the cabin where Marshal was sitting looking at his phone and Cristy was drinking a cup of something. She figured Alex was inside maybe taking a nap.

'You see Captain Sam's tattoo?'

'Yeah. Cool.' Minnie waved at Connie. Billy and Musto were heading down with a large jug and a stack of cups.

'Lemonade anyone?' They climbed the cabin steps up to the visitors on their deck. Minnie watched Cristy smiling and chatting with Connie and was pleased to notice Marshal thanking Connie for the lemonade without being prompted by his mom.

Sitting on the warm boards of the jetty they quaffed the cool tangy sweetness, watching Dan haul a length of sun-bleached branch on to the shore. He strolled over, wiped his brow with his shirtsleeve, and stood on the mud below the jetty, as Connie passed him down a cup.

'Look, erm ... we talked about this, but not much,' he began between sips, glancing up at the cabin to check he couldn't be overheard by the Ashton-Kittos. 'Not since, well, not since it happened.'

He had their full attention. 'So, is everybody OK? I mean, it's taken this long for it to sink in with me ... I kinda ... had to process in my mind ... what we saw.'

Billy looked down at Dan. 'It was real...'

'It *was* real.'

'No, it was real...' Billy was searching for the right word. 'Freaky.'

Dan patted Billy's knee. 'But profound, Billy, and important, and I think special. We all felt at peace when it happened, right? Well, *I* did. I felt calm, not fearful.'

Minnie, Connie and Billy all nodded in agreement as they gazed out across the bay at the islands, remembering.

Dan looked the boy in the eye. 'But they've

gone now, and won't be bothering us again, so...'
He ruffled Billy's already unkempt hair, as Connie
exchanged a glance with Minnie.

The three of them sat in a row, dangling their
legs off the jetty, as Dan stood, leaning an elbow
on the boards. They drank their lemonade and
Musto sniffed around the tide pools, mud and the
seaweed draped over the ash-grey rocks.

Dan placed his empty cup on the jetty.

'I mean, something like that never leaves you.
Never.'

The four shared a silent recollection of that
night. The whole clan of massive hairy beings
running and jumping off their jetty into the sea,
then swimming away.

Billy broke the silence. 'That one ... that one
who ... that one who came close, he...'

Minnie looked at her young friend. 'He what?'

'He didn't harm us,' said Connie, 'or look like he
wanted to.'

'He looked,' said Billy, 'kinda friendly.'

Minnie slapped his knee. 'Right!'

Billy continued. 'But, if they come back, we're
moving. I've discussed it with Mom.'

'No!' said Minnie.

Connie took her hand. 'It's OK, Minnie, we're not going anywhere. Billy, I told you not to bring this up.'

'But you said…'

'I said not to bring this up. I, for one, do not wish to move from here…'

This time Dan put a hand on both Minnie and Billy's knees. 'They're not coming back.'

'How do you know?' asked Billy.

'Look, here's an idea.' Minnie had been looking up the slope, studying the cabins. 'Maybe when we finish the new cabin, maybe, just maybe, if you agree, maybe you could move to cabin number one. So you're not so…'

'Isolated?' said Connie.

'Close to the spooky forest?' said Billy.

'It is not spooky!' said Minnie.

'That's not a bad idea,' said Dan. 'I could extend it. Make it roomier.'

'No, we couldn't … these are your only source of income.'

'We'd put yours up for rental,' said Dan.

'It's got the best view,' said Minnie. 'Folks would love it.'

Billy was looking up at his cosy cabin home.

'Yeah. Until some Bigfoots came and whacked on the side when they were chowing down on grilled fish, mussels, oysters and fries. I'm, like, really hungry.'

Dan looked at Billy. 'Like I said, Bill, they've gone.'

They listened to the waves slapping against the wooden pilings. Minnie looked at Connie, lips pursed, like she had something important to say and had been summoning the courage to do so. Minnie got to her feet. 'I have an announcement! I'm gonna make a potato salad. Whether you like it or not!'

Cristy spiked another spud with her fork. 'This salad is truly delicious. Thank you again, Minnie.'

The evening sun hung low over Bigfoot Island, and cottonwool clouds passed slowly by on the breeze. Dan and Minnie were sitting with Alex, Cristy and Marshal up on the deck of cabin number four as the three visitors ate.

'My mom's recipe.'

Dan pointed vaguely up towards the forest. 'Everything's grown in Minnie's veggie garden.'

'So, your mom built this place from scratch?' asked Cristy. 'Pretty impressive.'

Alex loaded his fork. 'With a little help from Dan?'

'With a lot of help from Dan,' Minnie answered.

Billy and Musto were strolling down the grass past the half-built cabin.

Dan twisted round to face Billy. 'Hey, you want some potato salad?'

'Nah, thanks! We've eaten. Fries! I had fries!' Billy sauntered over to the group on the deck.

Alex pushed his half-empty bowl away, took a slug of his beer from the bottle, laced his fingers behind his head and announced, 'I like to hunt.'

Billy leant against the deck rail. 'If ya see a bear, remember to stay calm, speak softly and back away, giving him the trail.'

'Er, thanks,' said Alex.

'Closed season,' said Dan. 'Come back in September.'

'Sure, I know, but what have you got up here? Mule deer, mountain deer, black bear, cougar?'

'Never seen a bear here, but...' started Dan in reply.

'Yeah, but if ya see one…' began Billy again.

'Wolf?' interrupted Marshal.

'Yes, wolf.' Dan pointed up at a rowdy flock of seagulls passing overhead. 'And herring gulls, plenty of herring gulls. Don't shoot *them*.'

Alex continued his list. 'Raccoon, skunk, snowshoe hare, grouse, ptarmigan, quail, pheasant?'

'And remember,' said Billy, raising a forefinger to help make his point, 'if it can blink, it's not a snake. It's a slow-worm.'

Alex had more. 'Snow geese, white-fronted geese, cackling geese, turkey?'

'Sapsucker!' said Billy. Minnie giggled.

'Excuse me?' said Alex.

'Sapsucker. Yellow-bellied sapsucker. Hear that?'

There was a distinctive faint drumming sound coming from the woods. 'That's a woodpecker, surely,' said Cristy.

The drumming stopped abruptly.

'Yes, but not that,' said Billy, as an even fainter whistle-warbling sound pierced the silence. He pointed up to the forest. 'That.'

Dan looked at Minnie as she stood and gazed up at the woods. It was the only sound. All other birdsong had ceased.

Dan glanced at the sea. 'Oh, look. Sam's coming back over.'

The black inflatable was heading across, Sam steering from the stern, the prow dispersing a shallow ripple of waves.

'Tide's going out. Let's go down, kids, and help him unload their gear. We'll let you finish your salad in peace.'

Dan, Billy and Minnie set off to the jetty.

'Go help them, Marshal,' said Alex to his son.

'I'm still eating.'

Crack. Faintly, up in the forest somewhere behind Connie's cabin something snapped. None of them seemed to notice the noise except Minnie, who paused, turned and looked up at the trees, then carried on walking down to the shore.

Sam handed the bags up from the dinghy. 'I've got about ten minutes before someone pulls the plug and lets the ocean out!'

Dan took the bags. 'Yeah, and there's deep channels here too, between the islands, so it goes out quick.'

'Yeah, there's tide rips, boils, even whirlpools between here and there,' said Sam, pointing back across to the big tree-covered island. 'Makes for a challenging crossing.'

'In a boat?' asked Minnie.

'Swimming,' said Sam.

'Who would swim that?' asked Dan.

'Not humans,' said Sam.

'Moose?' asked Billy.

Minnie nudged Billy. 'Good. Good suggestion, Billy.'

Sam stepped from the dinghy and sat on the weathered planks of the jetty. Musto was sniffing around the boulders on the shore, waiting for the water to recede so he could hunt.

'What, then?' asked Billy.

Sam pulled off his faded red cap, and scratched his head. 'Listen, what do ya know about that island? Been over there?'

'No,' said Dan.

'Well, they wait and watch for when the tide is small, the currents are weak and it's safer to cross. There's limpets, snails, crabs. So much protein over there. Cockles is a favourite food. I guess they suck 'em out.'

'Whose favourite food?' asked Dan, as he, Billy and Minnie stared at Sam, on the edge of their seat.

'Sasquatch.'

Minnie squeezed Dan's hand.

'Listen, I don't want you folks to worry. They're over there, not here. You got 'em here?'

'No,' answered Dan firmly.

'No. Good. They swim to find food. This is a narrow beach here, so not so attractive to them. They'd never swim this far. Over there is beautiful. Pink gravelly sand, two streams emptying from the high ground, wide beach. No people, no logging, no nothin'.'

He twisted round and pointed at Bigfoot Island. 'There's a saddle between the hills there, they could cross easy, to get to the straits on the other side. Caves there too, I don't doubt.'

'Why did you leave?' Dan asked.

'Last night – a roar like you wouldn't believe. Long … so … long … and loud … boy! Told them it was wolves. And this morning, in the sand…'

'Tracks?' asked Minnie.

'Tracks. Multiple tracks. Counted three sets.' Sam showed the size of the prints with his hands.

'Woah,' said Billy.

'Three of 'em walked along the beach together. One real small, tracks the size of ya feet.' He pointed at Minnie.

Sam looked back across at the big island. 'That yell … they was tellin' us to leave … so we did. Pronto.'

Dan looked up at the trio sitting up on the deck. 'Alex likes to hunt.'

'Does he have a rifle?' Minnie asked Sam.

'Oh, yeah. He brought all the gear.'

'All the gear…' began Dan.

'…But no idea.' finished Sam.

Dan lifted two of the bags and nodding up at the visitors. 'Kids, let's keep this to ourselves. They don't need to know what we know.'

'I can tell Mom, though? About Echo, I mean, Bigfoot Island?' asked Billy.

'Sure, we'll tell Connie.'

Billy and Minnie lifted a bag between them, and Sam took the other one. They walked along the wooden jetty and up the grassy slope.

Chapter Three

The next morning Minnie leapt down from cabin number one with her small rucksack.

'Ready! I have water and snacks!'

Swiping at blades of grass with a thin stick, she walked up to join Connie, who was waiting by the new cabin while Dan was finishing some work. He unbuckled his tool belt and lobbed it up onto the deck.

Connie grasped Dan's forearm. 'Can't you just hike along the road a-ways,' Connie said, 'and find a swimming cove, or…?'

'They really want to hike up the mountain,' said Dan. 'He's got a gun, we'll be fine.'

Connie tutted. 'A gun. Great. I don't like guns.'

'Dan,' said Minnie. 'I don't actually think it's a good idea to go up too far.'

'Don't worry, Min, I will steer them away from, you know, the Bigfoot hotspots.'

'OK. Good. We'll go the other way. Good. The other way, Dan, because these city folk, well, they can't be trusted to, you know, not just wander off!'

'Minnie, it's fine. We won't go far and I won't let them out of my sight.'

''specially that Alex.'

'Right. 'specially that Alex.'

Alex, Cristy, Marshal and Billy stood waiting at the standing posts near the veggie garden. Alex had a rifle strapped across his back.

'Why are you taking a gun?' Billy asked him.

'A gun, and bear spray,' said Alex, 'to protect my family of course, little man.'

'Hmm,' said Billy. 'Not hairspray?'

'Excuse me?'

'I always take hairspray.'

Alex looked down at the grinning boy and decided not to engage him further.

'Let's go!' yelled Alex, and they set off up the trail.

'Billy? You sure you want to go?' called Connie.

'Oh yeah, Mom!'

Connie looked at Minnie knowingly. 'Then I'm coming with.'

'Really?' quizzed Dan. 'He'll be fine with us, Con.'

'No, no, I'm coming. I want to.'

High pines and dark conifers crowded the trail on both sides. Billy and Minnie walked on slightly ahead of the others.

'So, what do we have here?' said Billy.

'Whaddya mean?' asked Minnie.

Billy gestured expansively with both arms. 'What are we lookin' at here?'

'Trees!'

'I know they are trees. I was not born yesterday. What trees are they?'

'What trees are they?' She looked at her friend askance. 'You don't fool me with that question, Bill. I know you're not an idiot!'

'I live by a forest-covered mountain, I figured it was time to learn a little about my environment. In case, you know, I'm ever asked.'

'Who's gonna ask?'

'Oh, you know, one of your many guests.'

'We've had three all summer!'

'Yeah, but things are lookin' up.' Billy pointed at the tree they were passing. 'What's this?'

'Fir. A fir tree.'

'Good. I knew that.' He pointed at the next tree. 'And this?'

'Also a fir.'

'What's happening here? Are we in a fir forest?'

'Connie! He's being annoying and weird!'

Laughing with delight, Billy raced on ahead, hotly pursued by Musto. Marshal hurried ahead, too, passing the adults.

'Not too far ahead, Marshal!' called Cristy.

Dan grabbed Minnie's elbow and in a hushed tone said, 'We need to head them off at the pass.'

'What?'

He glanced back at Cristy and Alex. 'We don't want them seeing any *signs*, do we?'

'What signs? Oh, you mean…?' asked Minnie.

'The footprints. The prints you found are up this trail. I'm guessing they're still there.'

'Oh! Right! Yes. No. Right! Billy! Musto!'

'They would get Alex really excited.'

Minnie ran on ahead, rounding a slight bend in the trail just in time to see Billy disappearing up their 'special' trail.

'Billy! Billy get back here!' called Minnie.

Marshal stopped, and looked back at Minnie. He picked up a baseball-sized rock and threw it into the trees. It *clonked* somewhere deep in the woods.

Minnie stopped and faced the boy. 'You could hit a creature doing that.'

'Highly unlikely,' was his response.

'Musto! Billy!' she yelled. 'Here! Come here now!'

'What is your beef?' said Marshal. 'Chill out.'

Billy reappeared with Musto from the game trail that wound between the low bushes and tall grass, both looking at Minnie quizzically.

'What? Why?' asked Billy. 'We always go this way. And I've got Musto to protect me.'

Minnie looked at the grinning dog. 'Not today. We don't go that way today.'

The adults arrived at the scene.

Dan put a hand on Minnie's shoulder. 'Yeah, there's poison ivy up that trail, so…'

'Yes, Billy, poison ivy,' said Minnie pulling his jacket. 'Remember?'

She gave him a look, raising both eyebrows, and Billy winked knowingly at her.

'Oh yeah, right, sure, I remember now. Poison ivy.'

Connie was the only one of them never to have actually seen the four massive footprints that had set the whole adventure in motion, and she leant down and whispered to Minnie, 'Is that where..?'

Minnie nodded.

'Should always stick to the trails,' said Cristy.

'Except when the trail is really boring and just goes, like, straight up,' said Alex, adjusting the rifle strap across his chest. 'Let's go down here. Checked this for poison ivy, Dan?'

Alex trotted down a steep but narrow trail on the opposite side of the hiking trail, where passing deer had flattened the long grass and pushed aside twigs and boughs. He quickly disappeared from sight into the thick undergrowth between the pines. The others followed him.

Minnie nudged Dan with her elbow. 'This is good. Down here is good. Better than going up.'

It was cooler in the shade under the leafy, low oaks and the path weaved between large grey boulders and stands of high-arching ferns. Minnie walked with Billy, behind Cristy and Marshal and in front of Dan and Connie. A pair of white butterflies appeared and accompanied Minnie in an erratic dance, escorting her down the path to a densely wooded ravine. The path levelled out at a grove of maple trees. The maple's grooved trunks were covered in yellow and green mosses and lichens, and their big five-lobed leaves cast a patchwork of shade on the forest floor.

Emerging from the maple grove, the group was stopped in its tracks by a magical-looking forest clearing. Midges, moths and flies circled and darted about in the shafts of sunlight that sliced brightly through the leafy canopy. Wisps of grey-green lichen looped and trailed from the lower boughs of the ancient wide-trunked cedars and hemlocks, and thick clumps of pale-yellow moss covered the grey-brown trunks of tall, straight cottonwood trees. Scattered clusters of ferns, some as high as Dan, dotted the damp forest floor, their arching green feathery fronds rising stiffly from the earth.

Connie ran her hand up a tall stem. 'Just look at these ferns! They love it shady and moist.'

'This is beautiful,' said Minnie. 'Why've we never come this way before? It's like a magical ferny grove!'

'Yes,' said Dan. 'I guess we always headed up instead of down.'

They proceeded on down the trail.

'What are those, Connie?' Minnie pointed at a clump of broad green leaves.

'Oh, skunk cabbage.'

Minnie reached up to touch the waxy-sheen of

the leaves, standing on thick stems like flags unfurled waiting for a breeze.

'They don't smell, Connie.'

'In the spring they have a yellow flower that stinks. The bugs love it.'

At the head of the walking group, Musto and Billy came to a halt in front of a massively wide, and impressively twisted old tree. It had distorted bulges and knotty burls growing out of its trunk a few feet off the ground, with five weird thin branches sticking directly out of the swelling like splayed, spindly fingers.

'Wow. That is centuries old,' said Dan. 'Red cedar. So that means all these hemlocks and firs are likely centuries old too.'

'That's gnarly,' said Marshal, pointing at the tree.

'There's more,' said Alex. 'Look.'

There were dozens of them – twisted, knotted, bulbous trunks of ancient trees as wide as majestic redwoods, their lower branches garlanded with long fronds of lichen left hanging like ghostly grey swathes of discarded rags.

Connie had stepped along a parallel game trail. 'Hey Dan, look at these trees! Didn't know we had these here.' The trunks were a deep, rich reddish-brown with shiny bark peeling away, like shaved chocolate curls.

'What are those?' Dan called from up the trail.

'Arbutus trees!' Connie stroked a shiny limb. 'Oh, and huckleberries! Huckleberries, guys!'

Cristy and Marshal walked back down the trail and began picking the blue berries..

'Oh, yum,' said Cristy.

'Billy!' called Connie. Billy ran back down the path and joined them.

Minnie loved huckleberries and hurried over to the bush. Though shady under the leafy canopy in the ravine, bars of sunlight highlighted the deep reddish-purple berries of the bush, casting a light so bright the green was almost white.

'Alex!' called Cristy. 'Huckleberries!'

Alex stood alone up the trail beside a wide, wizened cedar. He held his rifle at the ready and was scanning the trees, the undergrowth, the shaded bushes across the stream between the trees.

He gave Cristy a 'thumbs-up' without looking back, which she answered with, 'That's OK, your lordship, thy servants will gather bounteous fruits for thee!'

After gathering and eating their fill, they moved on. Marshal dropped back and fell in behind his mother as they walked silently along the trail. Alex followed, his rifle held across his chest.

Minnie glanced back to see Musto standing stock-still, his ears cocked, looking at one of the weird, wide, twisted trees. The hairs on the back of Minnie's neck stood up. A funny feeling instantly came over her, the distinct feeling she was being watched. She looked around at the bushes, the undergrowth, the ferns.

'Musto!' The dog snapped out of his trance and galloped up the game trail to her side. 'OK, boy. It's OK.'

Dan was looking back at the tree Musto had been interested in and Connie asked, 'What is it, Dan?'

'Nothing.' He walked on, resting a hand on Minnie's shoulder.

'All good?' she asked.

'Yup,' he answered, but Minnie knew something was on his mind.

'Here's a stream!' called Alex from up ahead.

'Ah, a babbling brook,' said Billy. 'Shall we pause for a picnic?'

'It's a beautiful spot,' said Cristy.

'It's creepy,' said Alex, 'too quiet.' They all listened. The forest had indeed fallen silent.

'It's not creepy, it's magical,' said Cristy.

Minnie too felt that it was magical and was beginning to quite like Cristy, even though sharing this forest and her mountain felt somehow wrong. And knowing as only she and Connie did, that there was a very large and powerful Sasquatch living somewhere in these woods made her uncomfortable. It felt wrong to her, with anyone other than Billy, Dan and Connie. Wrong to be in the woods at all, like they were truly trespassing on someone else's land. She felt at that moment that she'd be welcome in the forest with Musto and maybe Billy. Or, with Musto and Dan. But with all these people it felt wrong to her, and it *was* very quiet.

She whispered to the trees. 'I'm sorry.'

'Well, what can I say? *I* think it's spooky here,' said Alex who had paused and was waiting for Minnie, Dan, Billy and Connie.

'Alex. You're frightening the kids,' said Cristy.

'He's really not,' said Minnie.

Dan pointed with a stick. 'Maybe we should cut up back to the main trail.'

'Yes, let's go back,' said Minnie.

'Lead on, Macduff,' said Alex as he shouldered his rifle and let Dan pass him.

'Macduff?' asked Billy.

'From *Macbeth*,' said Alex.

'*Macbeth*?' asked Billy.

'Move, Billy. Follow Dan.'

Connie gently pushed Billy up the trail, her face an anxious mask, as Dan cut up the slope, heading straight up to the hiking trail.

'Go ahead,' said Alex, waiting on the trail brandishing his gun, 'and I'll bring up the rear.'

Hoping to ease the tension Minnie said, 'Hey Billy, he's going to "bring up the rear". Must be from *Macbeth* also.'

Billy chuckled, but Connie was not in the mood to laugh and glanced back at Alex, who was far enough behind them not to hear. Connie whispered, 'I am not enjoying this hike, Minnie!'

'You didn't have to come, Connie.'

'After what you told me, yes, I did. This forest is in lockdown.' Connie glanced about from tree to tree, shadow to shadow. 'Listen. Not a peep. Something's up. If I see that crow friend of yours, I swear I will freak.'

'What friend of yours?' asked Billy.

'What?' said Minnie. 'No one.'

'A crow?' asked Billy.

Connie gently pushed Billy on the shoulder. 'Please! Billy, hurry up the way there! Go on. This place is giving me the heebie-jeebies.'

'Heebie-jeebies! Good one, Mom!' And with that, Billy trotted up the trail.

They stood in a group on the main hiking trail as Alex emerged last from the tall grass and ferns, rifle at the ready.

'Down or up?' asked Dan.

'Down,' said Connie, passing Billy a water bottle.

'Down,' repeated Minnie.

'What's up the trail?' asked Alex.

'Goes pretty much straight up for a mile or so,' said Dan.

Minnie took a swig from her bottle. 'Yeah, nothing to see up there. Just trees.'

'Fir trees mostly,' said Billy. 'Yup. Mostly the good old fir.'

Alex straightened the pack on his back. 'Does it loop round back on itself, or...?'

'No, straight up and down. Same way up, same way down.' Dan gestured with his arm.

Minnie copied the swinging gesture. 'Same way up, same way down. Pretty boring.'

Marshal had already started walking down the trail. Connie took Billy's hand and they followed him.

'Well, it's hot and nearly time for some lunch, right?' Alex headed downhill with Cristy.

Dan and Minnie followed them. 'It's beautiful,' said Minnie, 'in that ferny grove, don't ya think? Did Mom ever go in there?'

'I don't think so. She never mentioned it.' Minnie took Dan's hand. He looked at her, weighing up whether to say what was on his mind. Minnie had consistently surprised him with her good sense, bravery and resourcefulness, so he took a deep breath and said, 'Keep this to yourself, Minnie, but I smelled something like that foul stink when that, that creature appeared by our deck.'

'They are people, Dan. Forest beings. Part human, part unknown species. I've told you that. I've done the research. Online.'

'I know, Minnie, I know you have.'

'Indigenous folk know, Dan.'

'OK, OK,' Dan said.

'So, where did you smell the smell?' Minnie asked.

'Near the tree Musto was looking at. No one else was close enough to smell it. But they've gone now, the Bigfoots, so, I don't know…'

They walked in silence for a while. Dan said, 'It's mighty quiet.'

There was indeed no birdsong and the forest seemed unusually still. Minnie thought she heard a short whistle like a *peep-peep-peep*, down in the grove they had just climbed up and out of.

Minnie pointed. 'Ah! I hear a bird.'

Moments later she caught sight of something out of the corner of her eye. Landing on a pine branch was Minnie's attentive crow-friend she'd named 'Caw-caw' – the same crow they'd found lying in some kind of trance on its back on their deck the night the Bigfoots had sneaked past the cabins.

Weeks ago, when she and Dan had been exploring the forest, after she had found the footprints, a crow had appeared. It seemed to be watching them and Minnie felt certain it was reporting back to the Bigfoots higher up the mountain.

The crow flew from the branch up to a higher branch of a pine tree nearby. It looked at Minnie with its beady yellow eye. In her mind Minnie said to the crow, 'Hey, Caw-caw. Tell him to stay up there.'

That afternoon Dan and Minnie worked together lifting floorboards up from the deck for the next level of their new, bigger and better cabin. They had a system worked out – Dan stood the planks on end, leaning up against a joist, then Minnie would hold the plank while he hurried up the ladder. He'd pull the plank up and Minnie would watch as Dan nailed them down over the joists. Minnie kept him supplied with nails, scurrying up and down the ladder in her bright-yellow hard hat.

'Great view from up here,' said Dan. 'Hey Minnie, how about a little draw-bridge at the back here, on to the little cliff for when I'm checking the solar panel and the turbine? But I guess, as the Bigfoots are gone now, we probably don't need one for, you know, safety. But it would be cool though.'

'Oh, Dan. Do you really think Bigfoots would come and knock on our back door? That's really not their style. They'd just sneak up to the corner post there and shake the whole cabin for fun.'

'Very funny, Minnie. Yeah, very amusing.'

Minnie sat cross-legged on the deck and munched her lunch of a cheese-and-tomato sandwich. She looked up at the mountain and wondered what her massive, hairy friend was doing at this moment. She hoped he hadn't come down to take a look at the strange new people, hoped he was not in the Fern Grove earlier, hiding behind a bush. She liked to think she could tell when they were close, but she wondered if that sensing depended on the Bigfoot, that maybe they could switch off their extra-sensory mind-zapping ability, or whatever it was, at will. That would be cool, she reckoned.

Dan drilled a hole for a long bolt, to brace a crossbeam, the electric drill's loud shriek ripping apart the serenity of the afternoon.

Connie was strolling barefoot down the grassy slope, a wicker basket in the crook of her arm, with Musto trotting beside her. She wore a wide-brimmed hat to shade her face from the high, hot sun.

'Ah, good. You've added the drone of the power tool to your repertoire. How I miss the simple clunk of the working man's hammer.' She smiled. 'You're making great progress.'

'Sorry, it's very antisocial, I know, but only two more drill holes and I'm back to hammering.'

Dan climbed down the ladder and took the sandwich Minnie was proffering.

Connie placed two apples from the basket on the deck and walked on down to the shore.

There was a yell from the rocks and laughter. The tide was beginning to recede, and Marshal and his mom were looking in the tide pools. Minnie and Dan hadn't had visitors here since springtime, when her mom had been too ill to help much and she and Dan had done all the cleaning of the cabins, the stocking of the log piles for the burner stoves, and the washing and drying of the bed linen.

It was a strange feeling to see people poking

about on the shore, having fun. But Minnie thought that maybe it would be OK after all, and that this family would leave in a few days, happy and content and none the wiser about her friend in the woods.

Alex emerged from cabin number four, in dark shorts and a T-shirt. He walked down the steps from the deck and stood on the grass. He waved at Marshal and Cristy, then turned and, looking up at the mountain, raised binoculars to his eyes, scanning the forest.

'Look, Dad.' Minnie was watching Alex.

Dan stopped hammering, 'What's he looking at? It's just trees. Trees, trees, and more trees.'

'Maybe he likes watching birds. He seemed edgy, nervous, on our little hike. Did you notice?'

'Yes, I think we need to watch him. He's unpredictable.'

The sky had darkened. A breeze kicked up the waters of the bay and the first of a million raindrops plopped on to the deck.

Chapter Four

Minnie was woken by sunshine glinting off the cut-glass stopper of her mother's perfume bottle. The rainbow refraction shone red, orange and yellow colouring her pillow as green, blue and violet lit her face. She tried to work out how the sun had struck the glass when it was on the other side of the cabin. She realised the door was open and the low shaft of sunlight peeking over the mountain was shining through the kitchen window and had found the gap into her little room.

As she lay on her bed, Minnie reached up and pushed open the back window. A breeze, laden with the warm scents of the forest, blew softly through the cabin. From the windowsill she lifted the pinecone and smelt it again.

'Still piney.'

She picked up a long, thin stick. When she and Billy had first discovered the footprints in the forest she had found this straight twig to measure

61

the length of the Bigfoot footprint. When she'd got home she had used a ruler to mark off the seventeen inches, the length of the footprint. She swished it about and placed it back on the sill.

Swinging her legs to the floor she dressed quickly. In the kitchen she grabbed a banana, peeled it, smeared some smooth peanut butter on a slice of bread and wrapped it round the banana.

She stepped onto the deck. It had rained most of the night, the constant pattering on the roof, like a crowd of crows tap dancing, had soothed her to a deep sleep. Up behind the cabins the conifers dripped now and tall grasses were bent low by the weight of the downpour. The bushes that dotted the mown lawn of open space between the cabins glistened. The clouds had cleared away to the north, and around the cabins the air smelt washed, clean and fresh.

Dan was working along the shore, pulling up yet more driftwood dumped by the tide. Minnie's mom had called it 'free fuel' and had collected driftwood all year round to burn on their fire through the cold winter months.

Minnie wandered down munching on her 'breakfast wrap'. A sea fog was parting here and there as the sun inched higher, and through the wafting mist loomed the bent trees of the small nearby islands. The *Squamish Queen* was anchored a short distance out, resting midway between the end of the jetty and the closest of the islands.

Sam could be seen giving the small sky-blue pilothouse a fresh lick of paint. He had a fishing rod propped up nearby with a line dangling in the water.

A coolness rose from the sea on a gentle breeze hushed in from the bay. Seagulls called, and a flock landed far out beyond the boat on the glassy flat water like confetti on a puddle.

On a smooth boulder, statue-like, was a solitary heron. He was tall, with folded grey, untidy wing feathers, standing on one spindly leg, his black head feathers slicked back and a long dagger-sharp yellow beak pointing down at the mud.

'This is as close as I wanna get! Too shallow!' called Sam. 'You wanna swim out?'

Dan looked up from his pile of logs. 'No! Not really!'

'I do!' Minnie ran down the grass towards the jetty.

'Wait for me!' yelled Billy.

'No, Billy, you are not swimming out there!' Connie was carrying a small picnic basket and a cooler box, ready for their trip on the boat.

Dan waved up to Cristy, sitting on the deck of cabin number four. 'Hey, you guys care to join us on a jaunt around the bay with Sam?'

Cristy waved back. 'Thanks, but they went up the mountain. Left early. Won't be back 'til afternoon, Alex reckoned.'

Dan stopped. 'They went up the mountain?'

Minnie, in the process of pulling off her jeans, stopped still.

'Yeah, they took a rifle and bear spray...'

Minnie turned and looked back, as Cristy added, 'Hey, he's a frustrated big game hunter, so...'

'It's the closed season, isn't it, Dad?'

'Yes. As we discussed with Alex, the season opens in September.'

'He said something about fallow deer.' Cristy was coming down the wooden steps from the deck now, looking concerned.

'Did he? Well, it's correct that fallow deer are not a native species, and can be taken at any time, but we don't have them here. Only black-tailed and white-tailed deer.'

'Oh,' said Cristy.

'D'you think he knows the difference?' asked Dan.

'One's got a black tail?' offered Billy.

'He's a TV exec from LA. I doubt he knows the difference between a coyote and a wolf!' called Cristy, now standing at the wooden rail.

'Did he say where they were headed?'

'No, but he kinda pointed off to the left there.' She pointed up at the forested slopes. 'Like, he thought the fallow deer would kinda, like, be there?'

Dan put his hand on Minnie's shoulder. She was pulling her jeans back on, 'Let's go.'

They marched up towards their cabin. Minnie's heart was pounding. It was happening. Exactly as she had feared. A man who thought he was a hunter, but didn't really know what he was doing, had gone off into the forest with a gun.

'Hey, where are you going?' called Connie.

'To stop Alex from shooting anything!' called Minnie.

Billy stood in his superhero pose – feet apart, his fists on his hips.

'You need me to come?'

'Nah, Bill, we need you to hold the fort,' said Dan.

'Yup. Uh-huh. Copy that,' said Billy. 'Hey, take Musto!'

The shaggy yellow dog lifted his head when he heard his name and, knowing he was needed, bounded down the slope to Minnie's side.

Dan's rifle was slung over a shoulder by its leather strap. Shoved in one of the side pockets of his small backpack was a can of bear spray, black with a bright-orange safety tag. Minnie walked beside him up the track past Connie's cabin to where Alex and Marshal had left dark footprints in the still damp grass.

'How are we going to find them?'

'Well, Min, we may be able to follow their tracks if they cut up a game trail.' They listened to the forest and the rhythmic *clomp* of their boots on the hard-packed earth of the trail.

Minnie could sense Dan's reluctance as they strode on, and something else – perhaps for her he was putting on a brave face. She wondered whether she should tell him what she'd told Connie.

'I hope he doesn't shoot anything,' said Minnie.

'He's only allowed to shoot fallow deer, and there are none here on the mainland. We told him that!'

'Hunters!'

Dan put his arm round her narrow shoulders. 'You know hunting licences are issued to help manage animal numbers. It's all about balance.'

'I know, but… Well, maybe they should just let the Sasquatches balance the forests and stop the hunting.'

'Well, all our Bigfoots have left!'

Minnie glanced at Dan. 'Up there is theirs,' said Minnie. 'Down here is ours.' They walked in silence for a while. 'Dad?'

'Yup?'

Minnie sometimes called her stepfather 'Dad'. He had been 'Dan' all the years she'd known him, since he'd arrived to help her mother build more cabins, until recently. Until her mom had passed, and after the Sasquatches had banged on the cabin wall, pushed over tress, whooped and hollered in the woods, run past them and leapt in to the sea and swum away. That extraordinary shared experience had brought them closer together.

'How does that bear spray work?'

'You pull the orange tab then point it at arm's length and push the button, like an aerosol spray. It's got the stuff from chilli peppers in it, which stings their eyes for a while.'

'Oh. Sounds ghastly.'

'That's the idea.'

A symphony of birdsong filled the woods as they walked deeper into the forest, a constant whistling, trilling sing-song from the towering pines, cedars, and firs on both sides of the track. A slight breeze twitched the tops of the younger saplings growing on the edge of the forest trail. The warm scents of the forest enveloped them – resinous pine and sweet odours from blossoming yellow and pink mountain flowers scattered beside the path, like an exhalation from the warm earth beneath their feet.

'Maybe our poison ivy ruse will have kept them off your special trail,' said Dan, as they reached the point where the game trail cut up to the left, and where Minnie and Billy had found the Bigfoot footprints. They stopped and crouched down looking at the ground.

'I don't see any boot prints in the grass, Minnie. Do you?'

'No.'

They walked a little way up the special trail, scrutinising the ground for sign of recent human passage. Their feet crunched softly on the leaves and twigs, with Musto sniffing ahead.

'I can't see the footprints,' said Dan.

'They're further up.'

Minnie went on. She pointed at the ground. 'Here.'

Dan knelt to inspect the indentation, brushing pine needles and leaves away.

'Wow,' said Dan. 'I'd forgotten how enormous they are. Hey, I never noticed they're slightly pigeon-toed.'

'Oh yeah, they turn in slightly.' Minnie slipped her red backpack off her shoulders and pulled out the thin stick with the inches marked on it.

'Enormous,' Dan said again.

'Yes, and he's not yet fully grown.'

'How on earth do you know that?'

'It's still quite slim. The foot.' She was positioning the stick beside the print. 'It'll get wider as he matures.'

Dan looked at Minnie.

'Hey, I've been doing my research.'

'You kept that stick?'

'Yup. This was probably the young one, you know, the one who revealed himself to us that night. Seventeen inches exactly.'

'That was a young one? His head was twice as wide as mine!'

Minnie recalled the moment again, like she did many times every day even without trying. Those black, human-looking eyes – set wide apart above a flat nose, under a heavy brow of grey skin, with short reddish-brown hair growing low on the forehead – were never far from her thoughts.

'I don't think they came this way,' said Dan. 'Let's go back and walk further up the trail. Come, Musto!'

They re-joined the main hiking trail and Minnie regarded the forested mountaintop ahead of them, which never seemed to get any closer, no matter how many paces they took towards it.

70

'Boot prints.' Dan was pointing at the ground. 'Where the gravel gives way to soil.'

'Good thing it rained,' said Minnie.

'Yup.'

'How long do you reckon to get to the top?' she asked.

Dan looked up at the broad peak where, at one end, a prominent dark-grey granite outcrop broke up the conifers.

'Oh, I don't know, maybe an hour or so. Or thirty minutes if you run.'

'Ha! No one could run up that!'

As they walked higher, it seemed as if they had left the birds behind. Every last peep and whistle of birdsong, the soundtrack to the forest, had faded. In the deafening silence Minnie said, 'It's gone very...'

BANG!

A gunshot rang out, ripping the silence apart. It wasn't close, but it was near enough for its echo to resonate through the forest.

KAAYII

Chapter One

High up in a pine tree on the ridge near the summit of the mountain, Kaayii sat on a stout branch, hugging the slender top of the trunk, as the wind gently swayed his tree and all the lofty tops of the pine trees in the forest on the mountain. His huge, hairy black hand waved away a friendly bee that landed on his wide grey nose. The buzzing insect circled his head and landed by the notch in his right ear. Kaayii brushed the bee away and touched the notch with his fingers, remembering the fight in which the enormous wolf bit his ear.

The wind made his black eyes water. He blinked. Across the bay, near the large, forested green island, something was moving on the water. If he had been looking across at the far end of the pond in the meadow near his cave, and if a small white petal had landed there, it would have been about the same size. This white speck was so far away he could not make out what it was, but it seemed to be very slowly getting bigger.

He glanced far down the sweeping tree-covered slopes to the base of the mountain and the shoreline of the bay. He could just make out a thin white line of breaking waves on the rocks and the wooden jetty where, a while ago, he had left seafood for the human girl with the curly brown hair. He'd first seen her not far from the Watcher's Place, where she and the small boy had found his footprints on a game trail, and he had watched them from a low ridge through a tangle of uprooted trees and loose brush.

Their friendly shaggy-haired dog had locked eyes with Kaayii through the undergrowth that day, but the dog and the girl didn't communicate like other creatures did and the dog could not tell her what he'd seen, so she had had no idea that the young Sasquatch was there, lurking.

He studied the area around the cabins hoping for a glimpse of her, or even of the dog. The sticky pine resin on his fingers reminded him that his mother had smeared a piney mixture on the girl's head when she'd fallen and cut her head while walking in the woods a few days later. When he'd found her asleep on the ground, he had knocked loudly on a tall pine tree three times with a stout stick to call his mother and father down to join him from High Ridge, where they'd made their clan's den.

He'd often thought about the girl and her small clan, in the days since his own clan had left for the island. He hoped the humans had friends, friends who visited them often. Kaayii hadn't had visitors but he had his two wolf friends for company.

Climbing slowly down the tree, his huge back and shoulder muscles bunched and rippled under the thick reddish-brown hair covering his body. Though only few years older than Minnie, he was built like a seven-feet-tall prodigiously powerful giant. He hung from the lowest branch and dropped to the ground. He whistled for the wolves, sensing they had moved down the mountain.

This place, the highest ridge on the mountain, covered in fir and pine trees, had been the clan's home after the fire had driven them from their land. At the edge of the ridge, just within the treeline, Kaayii stared eastwards across the ravaged landscape. The scorched earth was charred black and ashen as far as the eye could see. Many trees were still standing but stripped of their branches, looking like slim black sticks. There were occasional wisps of smoke still twisting up from a smouldering patch of ground.

The range of darkened hills was a night's walk away, or half a night's run. Somewhere there was the cave where he had been born and where he'd lived with his father, mother and sister until the fire had come from the east, moving as fast and furious as a winter storm from the west.

The structures the clan had made here on High Ridge, by pushing broken tree limbs together, had been dismantled when they'd decided it was time to go, as had the nest beside the fallen redwood where his grandmother had slept before she died.

Now, growing amongst the bright green moss that covered her resting place was a ring of small white mushrooms. He ate them as he thought of his grandmother, and stretched out on the soft mossy carpet next to the sapling they had planted on her grave.

He could still make out the footprints of his

family members in the earth, and could tell which belonged to his father, which to his mother and which were his little sister's. He gazed up at the pine boughs high above, wondering what they were all doing over on the island across the water. He knew there would be plenty to eat there, along the seashore, but he hoped that they had found a warm cave that was big enough for all of them to sleep, eat, and laugh together.

Each night as the sun set behind the hills on the island across the bay he stood and sang their names, low and slow, commencing always with his mother, father, sister and uncle. Yumiqsu ... Taashi ... Yaluqwa ... Ahniiq... And then the others in their group: Ahnoosh ... Yaaqwun ... Shumsha ... Wesh ... Enksi... And lastly his grandmother's name: Shweya... He repeated her name over and over.

The young guardian of the forest's song vibrated through the connecting roots of the trees great and small, through the subterranean fungal threads that laced plants and creatures together, and resonated through the air – the breath of the forest.

Stepping out of the treeline facing towards the bay, his long, muscular, hair-covered arms by his side, his immense black hands reaching to his knees, Kaayii took a moment to tune in to the energy of the forest, then set off running smoothly and speedily down through the high grass and meadow flowers to the nearest stand of tall pines and the even taller, wider ancient cedars, hemlocks and redwoods.

He ran, leaping and bounding over bushes, fallen trees and patches of dark, slippery mud, long hair flying out behind him. Sometimes for fun he would dive and roll on the soft compacted debris of leaves and bark on the forest floor, before springing to his feet and running on. The squirrels stopped to watch him pass and larger mammals going about their daily business heard, smelt or sensed the young Sasquatch and warily stopped what they were doing, holding their breath as he passed. On the slopes above and below him a herd of black-tailed deer, a lurking mountain lion, a massive bull moose, two raccoons and a porcupine quietly moved away, deeper in to the moss-draped trees, the tall ferns and the tangled underbrush.

Down a ravine and up the other side he ran, the same ravine where the girl had slipped and cut her head. Descending the loose rocks in the next ravine, he slipped as a flat rock scudded out from under his vast foot. Deftly he broke his fall with a strong right arm and continued on all fours, galloping up the ravine, over a low rocky bluff, past the tipi-like structure of several tall trunks standing with their tops touching, and past the 'blind' he had built with his father and uncle. The blind was made from stacks of uprooted trees laid like a fence, one on top of the other, with brush piles and broken branches pushed on and around the stack. They could sit well-hidden behind the blind and wait quietly for older or sick animals whose time had come to pass into the next life.

Wanting to watch the humans, he didn't stop at the crystal outcrop up on the rise, but ran on towards the Watcher's Place, gliding by the Giant X made of two crossed trunks, through the stand of slim white aspens, pausing only to swipe up handfuls of the wild onion that grew there.

The Watcher's Place was where a delegated clan

member would sit and watch the lower part of the mountain. At his nest of pine boughs, moss and redwood bark, hidden behind a carefully woven web of twigs, branches and roots, he found his two wolf friends. Huff was sitting up, patches of brown showing on his black chest, his piercing yellow eyes alert as Kaayii came in to view, having sensed his approach. He twitched his broad snout, smooth and black with a few flecks of grey. Sitting by his side was the brown-eared, blue-eyed she-wolf – Mook, as Kaayii had named her.

Kaayii uttered a friendly greeting, 'Oosh,' and the wolves made space for their giant friend. He sat with his legs crossed. His vast chest and torso heaved slightly from the effort of running all the way down the mountain. He passed them the onions he had pulled and they chomped them greedily.

Kaayii had been chosen by his father to stay on the mountain, recognising his son's love for the dense forest from the moment they had arrived at the summit and feasted their eyes on the lush westerly slopes with the wide blue bay beyond, dotted sparsely with islands large and small.

Since he'd been made the sole guardian of the

mountain when the clan had left for the big green island, he had patrolled the slopes between High Ridge and the Watcher's Place daily, and sometimes at night too.

The smaller animals had been behaving themselves mostly, though pine martens, weasels and squirrels never really got along. As he sat in his nest, he looked about him and saw, about two throws of a pinecone away, a sleek, long-bodied, black and brown pine marten emerge from a hole in the curled trunk of a juniper tree. It leapt out, swiping with one arm at a tiny hovering black and red hummingbird. The marten narrowly missed the bird, which darted away. Running along a branch, the marten jumped up at a slowly passing moth, its jaws gaping and pointed little teeth bared. He landed in a pile of dry leaves with the moth sticking out of his mouth.

Kaayii knew that if the marten was hunting birds and insects instead of voles, shrews, rabbits, and chipmunks, the forest was still unbalanced, and it would stay that way until the miles of ashen, fire-ravaged land to the east recovered, and that time would come as soon as green shoots grew tall enough to feed the smaller creatures.

The fire on the far side of the mountain had driven more deer to the crowded slopes above the bay and Kaayii had allowed the local mountain lion and his two wolf friends to keep numbers down. The wolves, now fully alert, watched the pine marten, Huff's saffron eyes gleaming in the dense shade of the ancient trees where they sat. They contemplated giving chase, but were distracted by a *wump-wump-wump* from nearby scrubby bushes. Kaayii stood and could just make out the bright red 'eyebrow' of a grouse. So dark were its blue feathers that it appeared black, with a yellow and white neck. Mook *woof*ed once and the grouse's wings made a whirring *zwer* as he took flight.

Kaayii ruffled the fur at the scruff of Huff's neck, before walking down the game trail towards the trio of tall pines. The group of four pinecones he had left a few days ago was now just three. And one of his footprints in the earth had been brushed clear of the pine needles and leaves he'd scattered about to hide them. He knew the girl had visited and it made him smile. He had left the pinecones for her.

He grabbed a branch about eight feet off the ground and scrambled up one of the pines.

Gaining the higher branches, he had a clear view of the cabins down by the shore.

The white boat was over halfway across the bay. Kaayii studied the way a silvery curl of water split smoothly as it advanced. The girl's father was walking across the grass towards the jetty to meet the boat. Next to appear were the woman with the black hair and the small boy, strolling together in the gap between the firs and the pines. Now the girl came into view, hurrying after them. Kaayii smiled at the sight of the child.

Watching the humans was one of his favourite things to do. He'd been watching them while perched in this tall pine every day – their comings and goings on and around the water were a constant source of fascination.

He felt the girl was happier than when he had first seen her. He would know for sure when she was close enough to him to sense her energy better. He measured distance by how far he could throw a hard, green pinecone – though he would never throw a pinecone at her; that was the sort of thing his uncle, Ahniiq, would do for fun.

Kaayii spotted the yellow dog running on ahead across the grass between the cabins. It scurried down the low cliff to the beach and sniffed around the rocks, now with brown and green seaweed exposed. On the rocky outcrop behind the new cabin structure, bright sunlight flared off the four white blades turning in the wind.

Kaayii studied the half-built cabin. The humans had helpfully moved the old cabin that was standing in the way of the Sasquatches' ancient path, allowing his clan direct access to the shore, and the humans were now clearly building a new one, but it was taking a long time, probably because the man did not have a big family to help him.

Out on the water the white boat had stopped moving and Kaayii watched as four humans climbed into a much smaller black boat, which moved with a low buzzing like a bee across the calm water.

Kaayii smiled as these were surely friends of the humans coming to visit, and maybe they were joining them to help the man with his structure. He watched them clamber on to the jetty and talk – two men, one woman with yellow hair and a slim boy.

The girl with the curly hair did not smile though and was clearly not happy to see the visitors. After a short while she marched off up the slope, and up the steps to a cabin. Kaayii wondered why she was not pleased to have company.

There wasn't much bark left on the tree where he sat that he hadn't already peeled, but he found a stretch of it, and dug his black fingernails in to peel it back. Using his square white teeth to pull away the brown bark, he chewed on the succulent, creamy, inner layer.

Kaayii dozed, soothed by the sway of the tree. He was about to climb down and look for more food when the girl reappeared from the cabin. She walked up to the fenced-in garden, squatted down and began pulling and digging, digging and pulling. After a while, the woman with the long black hair walked up to join the girl, and they sat and laughed and talked together, until the woman stood up, now looking quite serious and worried, and walked up the track to the cabin nearest to Kaayii. Her cabin, he reckoned, was about one big looping pinecone's throw away from where he sat high in his tree.

When the girl left the garden and went back to her cabin, Kaayii climbed down the pine tree wondering what had worried the woman. One moment they were smiling together and the next she was troubled by something. Humans, he reasoned, and not for the first time, were strange beings.

Attracted by the increase in human activity, Kaayii crept furtively through the trees and the underbrush to get a closer look.

Standing in the treeline not far from the cabin of the woman with black hair, Kaayii could smell food. It was a sweet, burning smell and Kaayii began to salivate. The smell drew him closer and closer until he was standing by the back wall. There were no windows in the back of the cabin, but he could hear clattering and human singing from inside. He pressed one big black ear against the wall. He was so tall that his massive head, sloped from a slightly pointed crown to his enormous shoulders, was nearly at the height of the cabin's roof.

Inches from Kaayii, inside the building, the dog barked. It barked again, and he heard the woman speak to it. Kaayii moved round to the side and saw the boy and the yellow dog walking away down the track to the other cabins. So Kaayii, curious to see whether they were going to swim, or play, or climb a tree, followed them by crawling in a hunched-like creep on all fours, through the tall grass. He hid inside a thick juniper bush and, crouching low, grazed on the tangy purple berries.

Somewhere nearby a woodpecker drummed on a tree trunk. In playful answer to the bird, Kaayii made a particular Sasquatch sound, by letting his lips flap whilst whistling one sustained long, low note. After 'whistle-warbling' he listened for the woodpecker's reply. Turning in the direction of the woodpecker drumming in the forest, he directed his energy at it – though he couldn't see the bird he told it with his mind to stop, and it promptly did. He didn't want the woodpecker's drumming to draw attention to the woods.

Pleased that the bird had done as asked, because sometimes woodpeckers ignored him, Kaayii turned his attention back to the humans, whom he could hear talking on the other side of the cabin, up on the slight rise. He had had no contact with the humans since the night his clan left the mountain forest – he hadn't whacked any trees with stout sticks, he hadn't howled in the dead of night, and he hadn't mimicked any animal calls, and he certainly hadn't thrown any pinecones at them, or grappled with the friendly yellow dog.

Hungry again, he crawled out of the bush and slipped away through the long grass back up to the forest. Once in the trees he looked back to see the girl walking down to the shore with the others. He reached up and yanked down a low branch. It *cracked* loudly. The girl stopped and looked back at the forest. Kaayii smiled. Moments later the crow landed on a nearby bough.

'Oosh,' said Kaayii.

'Caw,' said the crow.

As Kaayii walked back up through the forest, he trod carefully, so as not to leave tracks, brushing past the waist-high green ferns, snatching up berries, and swiping up mushrooms when he saw them.

The smallest creatures were drawn to Kaayii, the largest being, and a shifting cloud of bees, bugs, wasps, moths and butterflies trailed behind him like a living cloak, dazzling and flickering, as he strode through the ferns. The only creature in the forest anywhere near his size, apart from a bull moose, was a bear. If a mature grizzly bear stood on its hind legs, perhaps while rubbing its back against the knobbly bark of a cottonwood tree, he would be as tall as Kaayii. A bear had lethal long claws instead of dextrous long fingers, and short awkward legs not built for sustained running, whilst Kaayii could run all day – he had legs like tree trunks and striding up and down the slopes never wore him out. He could also climb like a jungle ape and yell louder than a pack of wolves if he felt the urge.

As he neared the Watcher's Place, he clucked with his tongue twice. The two wolves had learnt this was their special call and came racing through the underbrush. They had wet blood smeared around their snouts and he knew he'd interrupted a meal.

All was quiet, as it usually was in the early evening – things got lively at night. He stood as still as a statue, feeling the energy of the forest. Bending down he grasped a fallen redwood branch in one massive hairy black hand and hoisted it on to his shoulder. Running up the game trail with the wolves, silently and swiftly, they passed through the stand of slim white aspen trees, their flattened leaf stalks twisting and fluttering in the breeze. Beyond the Aspen Grove was the first tree structure the Sasquatches had made when they arrived: a giant, perfectly symmetrical 'X', marking the start of their territory, that told other Sasquatches who might have wandered far from their own land that there were other beings living here.

The place had been chosen as there was a strong concentration of energy beneath it – a thick vein of quartz crystals under the ground that the Sasquatches could sense. The Giant X was connected to the even bigger crystal outcrop higher up the mountain by tree trunks and branches stacked in twos and threes, all connected to each other, laid end to end, to make a chain of energy from quartz to quartz.

He placed the redwood branch on top of a thin pine trunk that touched the base of the X. Kaayii had, in the last few days, added a whole tree stripped of its branches and shoved into the ground, its rootball upended. He had also created some 'ground glyphs' – symbolic twigs, arranged in triangles, squares and stars on the ground – that Sasquatches could read, each glyph representing a different member of the clan. Kaayii had positioned the glyphs of his father and mother and sister inside the largest square of tree trunks.

With the two wolves trotting beside him he jogged up through the brush, following the connected lengths of wood. Twigs and leaves had been blown on to the quartz here near the grey granite outcrop on the top of the small ridge. With his fingers Kaayii brushed debris off the crystal rock nudging out of the ground. A shiny brown centipede as long as Kaayii's thumb hurried across the bulbous quartz surface and scurried away under the loose leaves.

The crystal extrusion glinted in the evening sun, cresting the hills above the island. In places the crystal cluster was like tightly-packed small glass bubbles and in others it looked like straight shards of rusty brown and white, with clumps of dark moss growing in the corners and cracks.

He sat by the crystal rock, the two wolves curled up at his feet. He closed his eyes, wrinkling the skin of his heavy brow, as a large brown and black butterfly landed on his head. It was the size of a man's hand, so less than half the size of a Sasquatch's hand. It opened its wings to show white spots on the tips, and it stayed a while warming itself in the sun.

Kaayii decided this was a good place on the mountain to concentrate his feelings and send love to his father, mother and sister across the water. He knew that they would be feeling the love he had in his heart right now, at this very instant. As he thought of them the butterfly flapped and lifted away.

Chapter Two

The cave Kaayii called home used to be the den where a pack of wandering wolves from the north had sheltered. He and his clan had chased them away as they were killing too many animals on this side of the mountain. The wolves had also migrated ahead of the flames, across the charred slopes, but they were too many and their leader, the giant male who had torn Kaayii's ear, led them away to find new hunting grounds. Wolves can run many miles in a day and they would be far, far away by now.

Sitting in the cave on a pile of dry grass and pine boughs, Kaayii waited. Every day small animals would visit the cave. Some stayed and sheltered, most brought offerings of food. There was one cavernous space near the entrance to the cave where Kaayii could stand up straight, but deeper in where it was warmer the roof was lower and he had to crawl on his hands and knees. As he sat near the entrance there was a snuffling and shuffling as a porcupine waddled in. It stopped when it saw the two wolves but Kaayii told the porcupine, by the power of thought alone, not to be afraid. It turned around – stuck to its white-tipped quills were fat brown mushrooms. It reversed towards the Sasquatch who gratefully plucked them off and collected them in a pile. He thanked the porcupine, which hurried away, out of the cave. The wolves didn't care for mushrooms, but Kaayii guzzled them down. His belly full, he lay down to sleep.

Sasquatches don't bother themselves with the past and the future – they live in the present. Their future and their past visit them as ideas and memories only in the landscape of dreams. As he slept that night a memory floated by – a memory of something important that the Sasquatches had forgotten in the rush to flee the forest fire. Tied to that memory was a moment yet to come when Kaayii saw his father with him standing on a far shore looking back at this very mountain.

He woke up slowly, the vivid threads of the dream holding him with a sense of dark foreboding, of impending danger. He felt that he knew what he had to do, where he had to go, but he didn't know why.

It was not yet dawn; there was no light from the cave entrance. He smelled the wolves curled up next to him, Huff by his back and Mook close to his chest. Kaayii grunted and they both sprang to their feet and trotted out of the cave.

Where he was going, where he *had* to go, there would be very little to eat and it would take most of the day to run there. For the first time in many days he very much wanted to swim in the sea, to be weightless in the water, and to sample the sea's delicious bounty, to eat his fill before embarking on his quest.

Crawling from the back of the cave into the large cavern, Kaayii stood tall and stretched and yawned. The cavern echoed with his groan and a grey furry head with black bandit-like markings on his face popped up from behind a rock. The raccoon hurried out of the cave before the wolves returned, its black-and-white ringed tail flicking in annoyance at the rude awakening. Kaayii followed, emerging from the opening in the base of the granite cliff, to stand in the pre-dawn dark, among the boulders, behind the curtain of vines which hung from the rocky bluff.

The two wolves were drinking from the pond as Kaayii strode through the flower meadow under the stars. The bellowing call of bullfrogs ceased when Kaayii approached the water. He knelt, stuck his head in and sucked up huge mouthfuls.

The trio trotted past a stand of willows beside the stream, following it as it trickled over and under rocks, pooling briefly in the level ground, where deer prints showed in mud. The shallow stream led down through the pines and oaks, under moss-blanketed logs and fallen trees and after a while, as the sides of the ravine grew steeper and the gully deeper, the temperature dropped and the density and height of the ferns increased. The trees were much wider here, tall hemlocks and vast yellow cedars with twisted, bulbous trunks and low branches draped with trailing lichen, like ghostly grey beards. Kaayii found tightly curled new fern fronds and snapped them off, chewing on the juicy greenness.

The stream flowed through a wide pipe under the road at the bottom of the slope before emptying into the bay. Kaayii stood behind a hemlock tree and waited, listening. He felt it was still too early for humans, but the sky in the east behind the mountain was beginning to show the slightest tinge of silvery grey. He crossed the road in two bounds and jogged down the dusty path that led to the shore.

The wolves paced and watched as Kaayii sunk under the surface. Relishing the sensation of being held by cold, cold water, Kaayi could hear the sound of his heart beating and the whooshing, fizzing and popping of water in his ears. He floated, weightless and timeless and happy.

Searching between the rocks with his hands he found what he was looking for and pulled loose several lengths of wide slippery sea kelp, hurling the brown strands onto the shore. Knowing he'd need much energy for the day he stood in the water, focusing his mind and radiating calm, with his open hands hanging loose in the sea. A fish brushed his hand and in a *whoosh* he scooped it up and out of the water, throwing it onto the grassy bank to the waiting wolves. They devoured it in seconds. He caught three more fish. He threw two over to the wolves and ate the third. He took a deep breath and, ducking under the surface, probed the seabed with his long fingers, coming up minutes later with big, fat, curling sea slugs, which he lobbed to the wolves as well.

As the sky lightened, he looked across at the nearest cabins on the little rise of land. If a human had come out on the deck at that moment and looked out, they would have seen a massive dripping human-like figure wading out of the sea with strands of kelp wrapped round his neck like he was Poseidon, the Greek god of the sea.

Kaayii and the wolves crossed the road and followed the stream back up into the grove of ancient, twisted cedars, gnarly cottonwoods and giant ferns, Huff and Mook trotting on ahead.

Something red caught Kaayii's eye, stuck to the trunk of an oak tree. It was round, like the wide, red tongue of a moose, and thick, like a slab of meat. He broke the fungus off from the bark of the tree, sniffed it, and nibbled at it. It tasted good. He ate the whole thing in two big bites.

Near to the oak on a damp patch of dark earth grew a tree with small glossy green leaves and fat purple berries. He strolled over and began picking handfuls.

'Goompoop,' he mumbled appreciatively, as he

popped them in his mouth. Stretching out on the mossy floor behind a clump of lime-green ferns, the purple juices staining his lips and round his mouth, he closed his eyes and took a nap … for three hours.

Nearby human voices dragged him from his sleep. He was hidden between two heavily grooved red-brown cedars and the oak tree where he'd found the red fungus. The ferns were chest high, and the berry bush was between him and the game trail.

It was the girl, he could sense her energy, but she was with others, many others. He stood up, keeping a lookout for the people, who were still out of sight. He backed deeper into the undergrowth. He was so tall that his head brushed a branch, dislodging some hanging grey lichen, which sat on his head like a small grey wig.

He could see them now – the girl, the small boy, the girl's father, the boy's mother with the long black hair, but also their friends from the boat – the tall boy, the other woman, and the man who, to Kaayii's alarm, was holding a killing stick.

The small boy's mother stopped near to Kaayii's hiding place. She'd seen the berries. She called to the others and was joined by the tall boy and his mother. Then the small boy's mother called out again, 'Billy...' and the boy came running.

Kaayii wondered if that was his name. The boy's mother then called out, 'Minnie'. But next the woman called out an utterance that sounded like *hukkoobay*. The girl trotted over and began to pluck the berries. Was her name Hukkoobay? He thought back to the time he and his uncle Ahniiq had been watching over her, after she'd fallen and cut her head and had slept under the tree, while during the night the Sasquatches had kept forest creatures away from her, including a very hungry mountain lion. He remembered how in the morning, the man, her father, had found her and had been calling out one word. *Minnie*. It was the same word the woman with the black hair had just called to her. So *that* was the special girl's name, 'Minnie'.

The woman held up a fat berry in the fingers and thumb of her hand and called again to one of the humans, 'Hukkoobay!' Now he understood – that was the human word for the sweet purple berry.

He was pondering all this when he became

aware that the smelly yellow dog had seen him. The dog stood by the bush, head up, alert, looking directly at Kaayii. Using mind-speak Kaayii instructed the dog to *go away from here*.

The humans moved away up the path, but the dog stood his ground, his head tilted to one side, until the girl Minnie called out the human word for yellow dog, 'Musto!', and it looked away and ran off after her. Kaayii thought about these strange words – Billy, Hukkoobay, Minnie and Musto, and how very simple these humans were, simple and strange.

Minnie's father stood still by the oak tree, not far away. He hadn't moved. With his mind Kaayii told him: *go*, but the man did not go. Although he wasn't looking directly at Kaayii, he was transfixed by something. Kaayii knew that he was very hard to see against the background of undergrowth he'd chosen to stand in, but something was holding the man's attention. Kaayii wondered about it. He knew humans had no sense of smell compared to other animals of the forest, and Kaayii didn't smell of anything except maybe sweet berry juice and seawater. The girl called something and the man moved away.

Kaayii was relieved they were going. He had a long way to travel today and he hadn't meant to doze as long as he did. He wondered if eating all the red tree fungus had made him sleep so long.

He waited, watching the people move away up the trail between the noble trunks, through dappled patches of sunlit ferns and tall stiff grasses, as bees and flies and moths spiralled and dived hither and thither in the shafts of light.

When he could sense the humans were a safe distance away, and their voices had faded into the forest, he made a piping whistle sound, three short peeps, and in a few moments the crow landed on a low bough in the shadows of a wide old cedar. His shiny black feathers folded back, his vivid yellow eyes flashed in the low morning gloom, deep in the grove of ancient trees, as Kaayii told it by thought, to keep watch over the humans. The crow cawed once, and promptly flew away.

Chapter Three

Kaayii, Huff and Mook climbed the steep, rock-strewn slope up to the bare granite bluff shouldering out of the mountain above the cave. Across the charred ashen landscape stood mile after mile of skeletal blackened trees. Gusts of wind lifted swirls of grey ash, rising and twisting like the ghostly veils of invisible dancers.

The sun neared its zenith in the sky as clouds gathered in the east over the far mountain range, its peaks capped with snow even in the height of summer. Ash clung to the travellers and Kaayii, scarves of sea kelp flapping behind him, was well camouflaged within the grey landscape, even in the afternoon sun.

Gaining the flatter land, Kaayii jogged at a steady pace, the wolves either side of him, churning up small black clouds of ash.

Kaayii's father had stood with him and pointed from High Ridge across the fire-ravaged lands to the range of hills where their caves were. That fixed point in the distance guided Kaayii. They ran all afternoon. The open country, devoid of its tangle of undergrowth, thorn bushes and brambles, was easy to traverse. Only sparse patches of pale purple fireweed added colour to the spoiled landscape. There were no game trails to follow, but the fire had flattened the way and the trio loped on at a steady pace.

Apart from birds passing high in the sky, the only living creatures crossing the stillness of the dormant forest were ants, beetles, flies, snakes and worms that had emerged from subterranean holes deep below the ash.

Kaayii ripped off lengths of sea kelp and shared it with the wolves. Shallow streams with a grey scum floating on the surface flowed in some of the gullies and ravines. As the Sasquatch and the wolves drank the water, the ash stuck to the fur of their faces.

Droning high in the sky was something that looked like a dragonfly. It descended quickly and as it got closer Kaayii could see that the 'dragonfly' had a big round head. It was getting lower, larger. He realised it was one of the humans' flying things that had buzzed around when the fire was raging. The ones with straight wings would drop loads of water on the flames and once one like this huge black dragonfly flew so low he could see the humans sitting inside it.

He lay down and pulled a blackened tree trunk over him, scooping up armfuls of ash to hide under. The wolves stood and watched him. The noise from the 'dragonfly' increased as it came lower and lower. The down draught from it blasted up a sudden tornado of twisting debris. His ash covering blasted off him; he grabbed loose branches as cover and lay on his back watching the thing whirring noisily above him through the twigs. The humans had a good look at the two wolves cowering together in the terrifying cacophony of noise, then flew away.

A ghostly moon had appeared in the late afternoon sky and behind them the low sun kissed the high ridge they had set out from. They climbed now, the hilltop caves were close, and Kaayii called to mind again the day they had fled the fire.

The Sasquatches had stood together in the trees looking towards where the sunrise should have been through a thick haze of orange cloud. The wind, swirling about them like nothing he had known before, carried a deathly stench of burning. The older Sasquatches were yelling and screaming, and the youngest, his little sister Yaluqwa, was terrified and clung with all her strength to her mother's neck.

Sasquatches have no possessions apart from a favourite stick or club, or maybe an animal skin, so when his father Taashi yelled in their spoken language the words for 'run, run from the wind,' they all simply sprinted away down the slope towards the High Ridge in the west.

His grandmother had stumbled in her rush to exit the cave and injured her leg. His father had hoisted her to his shoulders and carried her down from the cave to the forest. He and his brother Ahniiq took turns to carry her all the way to the safety of High Ridge.

Sasquatches don't usually move in large groups, but this was an emergency. Two of the group would go on ahead and signal with wood knocks the best route to take. They had hoped the wind would change but it only became stronger. For two days and a night they walked and ran through the forest, keeping ahead of the fire but feeling its advancing heat in the wind on their back.

They saw no people, only machines flying in the smoke-filled skies. Animals ran with them in the same direction, all heading west away from the flames. On the first day he had seen moose, deer, rabbits, hares, porcupines, raccoons; even a mountain lion crossed their path. Creatures great and small were running, creeping, crawling, slithering and flying as fast as they could to flee the advancing curtain of fire.

Ahead now on the final slope that had once been their forest home, Kaayii found smashed trunks, tumbled together in piles. Looking around, Kaayii tried to remember how it had been before. He studied jagged rocks on the top of the rise, and he knew the caves were below them. The wolves decided not to follow, so sat resting as he climbed up and over the tree trunks and rocks.

The sun was below the ridge they'd started from hours ago, casting a shadow miles long. When Kaayii had climbed to the place where he remembered the caves to be, he lifted and pulled trunks aside. There was the entrance. It was only an angled crack in the rock face, but one wide enough for a fully-grown Sasquatch to enter if he stood sideways. This was the cave they'd slept in –

Kaayii, Taashi, Yumiqsu and Yaluqwa. He knew what he was looking for was in there somewhere, but he didn't know where exactly. In his dream his father had placed it safely on a high rock ledge.

Kaayii let his eyes adjust to the dark and moved carefully with his hands feeling the rough stone shapes of the cave walls. There it was – the shelf his father had reminded him of in his dream. He reached for it. It was too high. He stood on a small round boulder and felt with his fingers, probing in the dust. There was nothing there. He felt again. The edge had a raised jagged section of rock and was digging into his wrist. Snagged on the edge was some hair. Kaayii pulled it loose and, assuming it was his father's, he smelled it. It did not smell of his father. He hurried outside to examine the hair more closely. It was grey, with many of the hairs showing white in the dim light. His father had a few grey hairs on his chin and cheeks, but these were longer hairs. Kaayii realised at that moment that the object of his quest had already been taken.

In fatigue and disappointment, Kaayii faced the empty cave, a home now bereft of life. High above, slate-grey clouds smothered the stars in a gloomy blanket, and for the first time since his clan had swum away from him across the bay, Kaayii felt very much alone.

A movement in the fissure that led to the cave caught his eye, black and white stripes down the back of a small creature showing in the gloom. Kaayii crouched low on his haunches as the chipmunk shuffled out of the dark. Its thin tail lay red-raw and limp on the ground. It peered up at the young Sasquatch. A second chipmunk inched out of the shadow, its bushy tail intact, but with burnt, reddened feet. Kaayii swept them up in his vast hands and carried them as he negotiated the climb back down the jackstraw pile of tangled tree trunks to the waiting wolves.

As they walked and jogged through the night, each wolf with a chipmunk clinging to its back, half buried in the deep ruff of neck fur, a fine mizzling rain became a steady downpour. Black, ashy gloop stuck to their feet and clung to their legs. They splashed through puddles and waded across fast-filling gullies as the rain swamped the bare ground, water racing down slopes in thickening ribbons of black.

Chapter Four

It rained all night, only easing as the eastern range turned a thin shade of grey, hinting at dawn's arrival. They mounted the last slope wearily, gaining the high ground above his cave home, standing again where they'd stood the day before on the bluff by the granite outcrop, but now looking west, at the grove of pines below with its tangle of looping creepers, at the small pond in the flower-carpeted meadow, and the dark forest beyond.

They picked their way down the loose shale-covered slope and crossed the meadow. In the mud of the streambed below the pond, on the edge of the running water, which was full now after the night of rain, was an outcrop of quartz, bulging from its earthly vein. He held his hand firmly on the lump of creamy crystal, allowing calming energy to spread through his whole being.

He and the wolves crouched to slake their thirst by the cattails sprouting in great numbers, like so many slim green swords across the pond. As they drank, he could hear the stream tumbling through the rocks towards the lush grove and on down to the bay.

Kaayii lifted the chipmunks from their furry sanctuary and gently placed them under a large leaf near the pond.

Rainfall had washed the forest to a sparkling freshness, and as the early morning sun crested the mountain range, it caught the moisture on the dripping trees, and shone in silver flashes. Kaayii's long fingers brushed the knee-high flowers. The scent from the yellow blooms and the pine made a heady mix in the warming forest glade.

Cobwebs garlanded the bushes, bejewelled by rain. The place hummed with life as insects left shelter to go about their business yet, as he began to walk towards the trees, Kaayii recalled the danger he'd felt after his dream and now he sensed an unusual tightening in the fabric of the forest.

He and the wolves ran up to the clan's gathering place amongst the firs and pines on High Ridge. The stiffening breeze pushed the pines' upper branches, knocking them together as Kaayii stood by the circle of stones under which his grandmother's body lay.

Fear bloomed in the heart of the young Sasquatch as he surveyed the disturbance. Moss in the circle had been kicked about, showing bare earth beneath, and the sapling they'd planted in the centre had been pulled up. It looked like the grave had been slept on – it was flattened in places.

Kaayii tried to replace the moss, patching the gaps and pressing it down gently. Searching the bushes and tall grass, he found where the sapling had been thrown. He carefully replanted it. Standing with the wolves, facing the island across the bay, he again sang his grandmother's name.

He walked with the wolves down the game trails towards the first ravine, the ravine where he'd found the girl. Drawn to the quartz outcrop where the Sasquatch tree structures all began, he strode up the other side of the ravine, sensing again the shift in energy. Kaayii wondered if it was human, or something else…

Using thought alone, he told the wolves to go, to return to the cave. They both tilted their head at him, unsure that he really meant to walk the forest without them. He told them again, and they loped away.

He strode up the second ravine as quietly as he was able – it wasn't easy as the rocks were small, flat and loose. Joining the game trail, he realised the forest had settled to a hushed stillness. In his mind he called for his crow friend. He waited. Apart from the *shhh* of the wind in the pine needles, an occasional windy whisper in the trees, no 'caw' could be heard. He waited, unsure what to do.

Moving in closer to the crystal outcrop, he glimpsed something moving slowly behind the redwood, the biggest redwood in the forest. It was the man, not Minnie's father, but the other man, and he was raising his killing stick to his shoulder ... *BANG!*

MINNIE

Chapter Five

The blast from the gunshot resounded through the forest. Dan and Minnie froze. Minnie cried out, 'No!'

Hurrying up the hiking trail, quickening their pace to a run, they rounded a bend, then another, twisting through slim saplings, tall ferns, fir trees and pines.

Suddenly, from the underbrush in the trees up ahead, Marshal burst out onto the trail. Heading towards them, all flailing arms in a stumbling run, with a desperate look on his face, he managed to blurt out, 'Help! There's...'

Readying his rifle for whatever came out of the forest next, Dan took a few paces towards the advancing teenage boy. Marshal ran straight past them.

'Marshal! Stop!'

The boy skidded to a halt on the damp ground, stumbling and falling. He rolled twice. Squatting on his haunches, he gazed back up the trail. Minnie approached him, putting a hand on his shoulder, as Dan ran back towards them.

'What happened?' she asked.

Gasping, between breaths, Marshal's eyes crazed, he mumbled, 'Saw something … I saw … something… I sa…'

Dan grasped his shoulder, 'What? What did you see?'

'Did he shoot it?' asked Minnie.

Marshal, horror etched on his face stared past them and said, 'I don't know! We have to go!'

Dan crouched before him. 'Where's your father, Marshal?'

Minnie shoved his shoulder. 'What did you see? What did he shoot?'

Marshal rocked back on his heels.

'It was big. I heard a stick break, in the trees, looked over and … it was hairy. Dad yelled "run", so I did.'

'Was it … a bear?' asked Dan.

Tears welling in his eyes Marshal said, 'I didn't … I didn't look back.'

'Then he took a shot at it?' asked Dan.

The boy seemed in shock. He got to his feet, and began to jog away from them, down the hiking trail.

'Where's Musto?' Minnie was running up the trail.

'No! Minnie! Stop!'

Dan ran after her, and grabbed her arm. 'Go back with Marshal.'

'I have to find Musto!'

'I will find him.'

'Dad, I've got something to tell you.'

Dan took a deep breath.

'Well, it's not really a big deal, but, well, I thought you should know … the young Sasquatch, the one who said hi to us that night … well, I watched him walk back up here to the forest, that night. He didn't join the others. He didn't jump off the jetty and swim across to the island.'

Dan took a moment.

'And he's here? He's still here in the woods?'

'Yes. And I told Connie.'

'You told Connie?'

'I didn't want you to worry. But now I realise I should have told you. I'm sorry.'

Dan's eyes searched Minnie's earnest brown eyes, framed by a scattering of freckles, freckles inherited from her mom, Georgina.

"Said hi"? The "one who said hi"? Minnie, these are wild creatures we know nothing about!'

'They are beings, like us. Intelligent beings.'

'They are massively powerful whatever they are, and we cannot predict their behaviour!'

'That is an accurate statement, but we need to find Musto,' said Minnie setting off again, 'and find out what Alex just shot. He might have just *shot my Sasquatch*!'

Dan peered into the dense forest, its thick undergrowth shielding the interior from view. It all somehow seemed even more impenetrable and foreboding than usual.

'Let's find the trail Marshal used,' said Dan. A little further up, where Marshal had burst out of the woods, he called out, 'Alex!'

Minnie yelled, 'Musto!'

Dan pointed at the trail. 'Boot prints, look. Alex!'

Minnie listened to the forest. She called again, as loudly as she could, 'Musto!'

It was as they listened keenly for a barked

response that she realised that, apart from their boots scuffing the ground as they walked, there was a solid background of silence. She decided not to mention it to Dan – he had probably noticed it himself, but Minnie knew that when it went deathly quiet in the forest strange events usually ensued.

Stepping quietly, carefully, up the trail that threaded thinly through the shady understory of moss-covered trees and tangled bushes, Minnie glanced up. The sky was almost completely blocked from view by a dark canopy of branches.

Passing by an ancient massive redwood, Minnie touched the reddish-brown fibrous bark twisting up the immense trunk in deep grooves. She could see no insects crawling on the gnarled hairy surface. She wanted to see a creature, any creature, something, just to prove to her the forest was alive. It seemed to have shut down.

On the ground too she saw no sign of life – nothing moved between the perfectly still ferns, nothing was crawling, nothing was creeping, no ants were busying, no centipedes were scurrying about. No breeze was dislodging dry leaves and debris from above.

Pressing on in the silence along the ridge of a ravine, an even bigger monster redwood loomed into view ahead. Ferns grew from the base of the trunk having found a place to root in the deep grooves of the buttressed giant.

'Wow,' whispered Dan, 'that's gotta be close to a thousand years old. It's as wide as my truck is long!'

Minnie touched it. Her head tilted back as she sought its topmost branches. 'How tall is it?'

'About two hundred and fifty feet?'

The hush was broken by a minor commotion. A movement caught her eye in the limbs above. Two squirrels chased along a high branch disturbing the cathedral hush, loudly chattering, '*Cheek, cheek, cheek*'. They leapt to a nearby tree, scurrying up to higher branches, out of sight from the ground.

'What spooked *them*?' asked Dan.

He raised his rifle to his shoulder at the sound of footsteps, rapid footsteps thumping towards them, brushing aside the cover, further up the trail, out of sight behind dense tangled underbrush.

Alex burst into view running full pelt, carrying

his rifle in one hand. He wore the full hunter's outfit – olive drab trousers and a plaid shirt, a multi-pocket camo waistcoat and a red hunter's hat with earflaps.

When he saw them, he yelled, 'Run!' He sprinted past, a twisted expression of abject horror on his face.

Dan looked at Minnie, 'This is *so* not good for business! Quick! Go!'

He started back down the track after Alex. 'We need to ask him what he shot at!'

'No, Dan, we need to find Musto. And whatever it was he shot at might be injured!'

'These are wild animals, Minnie! And he probably missed!'

'We have to check.'

'Really?'

'Yes.'

'I'm not keen, Min.'

'We should check. Let's just check.'

So they walked on, Dan taking the lead, his gun pointing the way. The trail twisted and turned, up hillocks and down hollows.

'I think,' said Minnie, 'somewhere to our left would be that Giant X. Oh … what is that?' She pointed through the trees to their right, off the game trail about twenty yards away.

An ancient pine had a fresh splintered rip in its side. Dan had his rifle held at the ready and lowering his pack he pulled out the can of bear spray.

'Hold that,' he said, passing Minnie the can.

'Why?' she asked.

'In case whatever he shot at is still here.'

Taking her hand, he led her through the ferns towards the damaged tree.

They stood before the tree, looking up at the gash.

'Bullet. Powerful rifle. It glanced the pine, see.'

The wound exposed splintered creamy white wood where the bullet had ripped through the side of the tree trunk, blasting a chunk away.

'I see no sign of deer,' said Minnie, examining the ground around and behind the tree trunk. Dan lifted his arm.

'That's eight-foot high,' he said. 'That was either a big bear on its hind legs, a mighty tall deer, or Alex is a really lousy shot, right?'

Minnie was pointing at the ground. 'Dan. Look familiar?'

There was a footprint, a massive footprint. Air left Dan's lungs and his whole body sagged. 'Uhh…'

Minnie's worst fear took shape in her mind. 'Here's another. And more going that way! I don't have my measuring stick to check if it's him! What happened here?'

Dan grabbed her shoulder. 'We should definitely leave. Now.'

'Look,' Minnie was pointing at a fern. There was blood, a couple of dribbles of red on the fern leaf. 'He shot him! He shot my friend!'

Dan touched it. It was wet.

A strong sense descended quickly on Minnie, a powerful instinct that they were not alone, and that they were being watched.

Dan lifted his hand. 'Listen.'

From deep in the forest came a crashing sound, like something mowing through the brush. Multiple trees were being snapped, shoved over.

'Sounds like forestry work. There's no forest work allowed up here. Is that machinery?'

'No,' said Minnie. 'That's not machinery.'

A dog's bark in the woods nearby made them both look up.

'Musto!'

'We ... should ... go,' Dan said just as, crashing through the bushes and yelping madly, the yellow dog sprang from the underbrush. Minnie fussed over him.

The destruction, the clamourous sound of breaking trees, continued but seemed to be getting fainter, as though whatever was breaking the trees was moving away.

'Let's go!' Dan pulled Minnie's sleeve, and they ran back down the trail, Musto galloping on ahead. They didn't stop until they reached the hiking trail, and Musto was long gone, out of sight.

'That dog could not get home fast enough,' said Dan, as he pulled a water bottle from his backpack and passed it to Minnie.

Again, they froze, as a sound that Minnie and Dan were only too familiar with split the silence. The longest, deepest, loudest, roaring *hoowwll* filled the forest.

Though it clearly originated some way away, it resonated in their bodies, bringing tears to their eyes and chilling their bones. This was an anguished cry, seemingly laced with profound fury. Minnie couldn't move. Her body was paralysed with fear. Eventually, after many moments, Dan spoke, and his voice eased the fright that had coursed through her body.

'It's OK, Minnie... Let's go.'

The terror that had seemed to possess her began to subside slightly and she breathed again. Gasping, but weakened by the force of the sound and the intent that drove it, she dropped to the ground. Dan lifted her up and carried her down the hiking trail in his arms.

'What do you think happened?' asked Minnie, when Dan lowered her gently and handed her the water bottle.

'He shot something,' answered Dan.

'He shot my friend!'

'Minnie, he's not your friend.'

'Yes, he is! He saved me. We have a connection.'

'That does not make him your friend.'

'If I say he's my friend, he's my friend.'

'Fine.'

'Fine.'

They hurried on down the trail, Dan glancing back from time to time.

'Alex went into the woods looking for something to shoot!' said Minnie, 'It's his fault!'

Dan put his arm round her. 'Look, we don't know what happened. Your friend may be fine. There was not a lot of blood. The bullet hit the tree.'

Connie rounded a slight bend on the hiking trail, running towards them.

'Oh, thank goodness!' she cried as she ran to Minnie and held her. 'Dan, what happened?'

'Where's Musto?' asked Minnie.

'With Billy. What happened? Alex has said nothing. They are *really* shook up.'

'We need to talk,' said Dan, 'and find out what it was he shot.'

Chapter Six

When Dan and Minnie got down to the cabins Marshal was on the jetty pacing up and down. Alex was with Cristy looking at his phone over on the rocky rise by their cabin.

'Why is there no service?' he yelled at Dan.

'It cuts out sometimes,' said Dan. 'Tell us what happened.'

'Where's Sam?' asked Alex.

Dan and Minnie hurried up the slope to join them. 'Took the boat to Watson. I thought you were staying 'til Thursday.'

'Hey Marshal, you got service on your cell?'

Marshal looked up. 'Don't have my phone! When are we leaving?'

Dan touched Alex's arm to get his attention. 'Hey Alex, I need you to tell me what happened.'

Connie, Billy and Musto were hurrying down the grassy slope to the cabin. Minnie knelt to pet the still-agitated dog, his brown eyes darting back at the forest as he pushed against Minnie's legs.

'Oh, Musto, it's OK.'

She stroked his shaggy, yellow fur and pressed her forehead to his snout.

'What did you see?' Dan asked again.

'Yes,' said Minnie. 'What did you see?'

'Alex,' said Cristy taking his hand, 'tell Dan what you told me.'

But it was as if he couldn't form the words. He stood gazing at the deck and swayed, shifting his weight from one leg to the other.

'He said he saw a bear,' said Cristy, 'and fired a shot to scare it away.'

'A bear?' asked Minnie.

'Describe it,' said Dan. 'Slowly and clearly, please.'

Alex sat on the steps to the deck. He let his phone drop to the grass. He rubbed his forehead with both hands.

'This is important,' said Dan. 'We live here. We need to know!'

Alex was watching Marshal still pacing the boards of the jetty.

'It was standing … behind a tree.'

'We saw the tree,' said Dan, 'the shot you fired.'

'I didn't hit it; I fired to scare it away. I did not hit it. I didn't.'

'Why did you aim so high?' asked Minnie.

'Er … I don't know.' Alex looked like he was about to burst into tears and his hands were shaking. 'That's … that's where … where its head was.'

'Black bear, or Grizzly?' asked Dan. 'Know the difference?'

Alex just stared ahead in a kind of daze. Dan began to answer his own question. 'One's black, and the other's…'

'Grizzly?' offered Billy with a grin.

'Billy…' said Connie quickly.

'Hey, tryin' to lighten the mood here,' said Billy with a shrug of his shoulders.

Dan crouched down to face Alex, who was still staring blankly at nothing, 'Was it black, brown…?'

'Big,' said Alex. 'It was … so … big.'

Alex stood up, pushed past Dan, went into the cabin, and shut the door.

Minnie, Billy and Musto walked down from the cabin to the end of the jetty where Marshal was now sitting, leaving Dan and Connie with Cristy. Seagulls called directly above them, and then landed in a disorganised flock on the gently heaving sea.

'Hey, hi!' said Minnie. 'Mind if we join ya?'

Marshal didn't reply, he just shifted over slightly to make room. Minnie and Billy sat down. Musto found Marshal's hand and nudged his black nose into his palm. The boy stroked the dog's head.

'He likes you,' said Minnie. 'Hey, it's nice to have some people around.' Marshal kept his attention on the dog.

'Instead of Big…' began Billy.

Minnie quickly jammed her elbow in his ribs.

'Ouch!'

'Billy – instead of just Billy,' Minnie said.

Marshal gazed down at the water slopping against the posts.

'The tide's coming in. We could go for a swim if you like.'

'No thanks,' said Marshal.

'Bears are scary,' said Billy. 'But I've never seen one.'

'No, neither have I,' said Minnie. 'We could fish if you want. Off here, while the tide's in.'

Marshal just kept right on gazing at the water. Minnie looked quizzically at Billy.

'Say, Marshal, why did it take your dad so long to run out from the woods?'

Marshal turned his head and looked at her, 'I don't know.'

'So, this … this bear was standing on its back legs? Wow.'

Marshal kept looking down at the water lapping against the sides of the floating jetty, which shifted slightly as it lifted up on the water, and then settled down on its posts.

'Your dad wasn't sure of the colour but thinks it was…'

'Grey,' Marshal interrupted. 'Grey, with some white, and…'

'And?'

'And nothing,' said Marshal as he got to his feet.

Minnie and Billy stood up too and watched him walk back along the jetty.

'A grey and white bear,' said Minnie. 'Highly unlikely.'

Later that afternoon as the shadows from the pines reached up the grassy slope, and the sun was creeping along the spine of Bigfoot Island, Minnie, Dan, Connie and Billy were sitting on the deck of cabin number one eating pizza. Musto was curled up under the table.

'Well, he just keeps saying bear,' said Connie. 'But he doesn't seem convinced.'

'He's in denial,' said Minnie.

'Minnie, we don't know what he saw, or what happened,' said Dan.

'Mom, I think we should move down here as soon as possible.'

'Why, Billy?'

'Because that forest is alive with large, dangerous animals, like bear now, apparently. It was bad enough having a gang of Bigfoots, but they had the good sense to leave...'

Connie looked at Minnie; Minnie looked at Dan.

'But *bears* roaming around near the cabin? No thank you!'

'Not near the cabin,' said Connie.

'Near enough.' Billy shoved more pizza in his mouth.

'But our cabin is full of memories Billy, and...'

'Exactly, Mom! Memories. I'll remember my memories.'

They laughed.

Connie nodded in the direction of the cabins on the rocky rise. 'Our neighbours are not so jolly this evening.'

They looked across to the Ashton-Kitto's deck where the three of them seemed to be sitting in silence, picking at plates of food.

'Sam said he'd be back tomorrow morning,' said Dan, 'weather permitting, to take them back to Vardy to catch a flight home.'

Connie gestured with her glass. 'He really is not cut out to be a hunter, eh?'

'Neither is Marshal,' said Billy.

Connie looked at Dan. 'And he seemed so ... so rattled. I mean it was a bear not a ... you know what.' Connie touched Minnie's wrist. 'Minnie, you're super observant. Did you see anything unusual?'

Minnie glanced at Dan and said, 'Um, well...'

'Billy-Boy,' said Dan, 'you wanna fill the water jug for me, please?' Billy grabbed the jug off the table and went in the cabin followed closely by

Musto. Dan waited till they were safely inside. 'Connie, we saw footprints. Big ones near the tree.'

'And blood,' added Minnie, 'on a fern.'

Connie looked at them both, her mouth gaping. 'Blood?'

'Minnie's worried Alex might have shot her Bigfoot friend.'

'Sasquatch friend,' said Minnie.

'What? Why?' Connie reached across the table and clasped Minnie's hand.

'Because there was no sign of a bear,' explained Dan. 'Just giant footprints, then something smashing down trees... Sounded like machines clearing timber for a logging road!'

'And the howl,' said Minnie. 'You must have heard that.'

'I did,' said Connie. 'I did.'

After lunch Minnie was helping Dan with the new cabin, as he was updating Connie.

'Once this level is in, I'll build the frames for the walls, insulate them, then cover them inside and out, probably baton and board, probably yellow pine, then the beams for the roof, stick the windows in, and we're dried-in! Easy.'

Minnie tugged Dan's sleeve.

'Dan, I think we should go back up to the forest and look for my friend. See if there's a blood trail to follow. We didn't check if there was a blood trail. We could track him. I think he's in trouble. That's my feeling. Even though Marshal, said the thing his dad shot was grey, yeah? Can we, Dad? Can we?'

'Nope,' said Dan, without looking up from his work.

Minnie noticed three backpacks and three overnight bags sitting on the deck of cabin number four. Cristy emerged from the cabin and added coats to the pile. She looked out at the bay. Minnie supposed she was hoping to spy Sam's returning boat between the small wooded islands offshore.

'I thought Sam was coming back tomorrow,' said Minnie as she helped Dan and Connie lift a plank of lumber from the ground up on to the deck. Dan looked up and scanned the sky from Bigfoot Mountain across the bay to the far hills of Bigfoot Island. It was mostly cloud-free.

'Yeah. Sam said some weather's coming in where he is which could delay him. But that's the plan.'

'So how come they have their bags packed?'

Dan pointed to the island, where its hilly skyline was smudged by low wispy-grey cloud.

'Hey, is that your eagle, Min?'

High above, so high that it was hard to see, and hard to keep track of against the bright blue sky, was the silhouette of an eagle – large, long wings and small head. It was wheeling in elegant, looping arcs.

'It's getting lower,' said Minnie. 'Maybe it's seen some fish.'

As the eagle flew closer its yellow talons were visible, curled up under its fanning tail, and flashes of its golden nape caught the sun. The trio stood together as it swooped and rose, banked and turned, and swooped again.

'It's watching something in the water,' said Connie.

Minnie looked out at the water beyond the small islands and remembered the last time she had been that far out, when she was scattering her mother's ashes from the canoes with Dan. Her mother had always told her to face her fears in life, and Minnie had responded that she didn't have any fears.

Minnie watched the eagle swoop again and this time with a splash, it grabbed a fish from the waves. She thought she would love to be up high with that fearless eagle, but not so much on that choppy, cold, bottomless water.

'Wow!' said Dan, shading his eyes.

'Beautiful,' said Connie. The eagle lifted away from the sea and flew over them towards the mountain.

'Where's his nest?' asked Minnie.

'Woah … that weather's coming in fast,' said Dan. The water was getting choppy as a stiffening breeze from the west dragged the cloud over Bigfoot Island, pushing cresting waves across the glistening bay, towards their cabin cove.

'What is *that*?' shouted Connie, shading her eyes as she pointed into the late afternoon sun now fading behind the cloud over the island.

Dan looked to the sky. 'That is a Piper Super Cub Floatplane.'

A bright yellow airplane with long white floats instead of wheels passed about as high as the eagle had been. They watched it turn and come around again, this time much lower. Minnie looked at Dan. He was smiling.

'Do you miss flying planes, Dan?'

'Oh, only sometimes, Min. Only sometimes.'

The Ashton-Kittos had heard its droning engine and were all standing on the deck watching the yellow plane. Minnie nudged Dan.

He looked across, spying the pile of luggage, and said, 'You don't think…?'

The plane flew over the cabins, and they all waved. Billy came running down the grass with Musto and yelled up at it, 'Hey, if you've got any snacks, drop 'em now!'

'It's too choppy to put down,' said Dan, jumping down the steps. He ran across to cabin number four, Minnie hot on his heels.

The plane was turning to come round again, lower this time.

'Hey, Alex!' called Dan. 'Is this plane for you?'

'Yeah!'

'Why?'

'I want outta here. We all do.'

'He's missed his weather window to land. He can't put down! Look at the waves!'

'I'm paying him a heap of cash to get us outta here, so I think he will.'

'He might get it down, but he'll not get up

again,' said Dan, as Alex punched numbers on his phone.

'Yeah, this is Alex again. Can you patch me through to Pilot Mike? I see him. He's over us now.'

'Hey, he's flying a plane, not taking calls!' yelled Dan.

Alex just kept his eyes on the yellow plane, which was coming round again, quite low, just beyond the furthest of the small islands.

'Is he going to try to land?' asked Minnie.

'He's taking another look,' said Dan.

'Tell him to land!' yelled Alex at the phone. Marshal and Cristy looked very uncomfortable about Alex's desperate intensity, and Marshal went back inside the cabin.

'I'm not paying for a fly-by!' yelled Alex, kicking one of the backpacks in frustration.

Minnie, Connie and Billy watched this scene with expressions of utter bafflement on their face.

'Honey. It's fine,' said Cristy. 'We'll go with Sam tomorrow.' And at that moment the rain reached them – a mere sprinkle in gloomy half-light, quickly ratcheted up to a full-on downpour.

The yellow plane dipped its wings in farewell,

first the left, then the right, and climbed higher heading back the way it came. They all watched it go, in a tense silence.

Dan and Minnie walked back to the cabin and began collecting up the tools, putting them under cover. Connie and Billy were racing with Musto up the slope to their cabin as the rain crashed down in a definitive summer flash storm, as if to say, 'OK, that's it. Fun's over for the day.'

As Minnie lay in bed that night, she worried about her Bigfoot friend. There was nothing she could do except hope that he was not injured and that the blood was from something else or that, if he *was* injured by Alex and his stupid gun, it was only slightly. Though Marshal had said what he shot at was grey, she knew not to trust a description given by a person still in shock. She had read about people who'd had an encounter with a Bigfoot, but not a close-up encounter like Minnie, and who had convinced themselves it must have been a bear they had seen. Alex was so shocked he had ordered a plane to come and collect them immediately, and Marshal was so shocked he had stopped looking at his phone! Minnie pondered the amazing effect that these creatures could have on unsuspecting humans.

She thought about all the forest animals and wondered whether they stopped their nocturnal activities and took shelter when there was a storm, scurrying down their burrows, nestling deep in their nests, and hunkering down in caves, under leafy ferns and fallen trees.

The rain pattering steadily on the cabin roof soothed her to sleep. She dreamed of her mother. They were swimming hand in hand in an underwater forest, with fish swimming in shoals around the trees. A pair of seals twisted round branches and danced together, then swam quickly away. She knew it was her forest, here on the mountainside – they were swimming near to the Giant X by the Aspen Grove, near where the wild onions grew. Two Sasquatches looked out from behind a redwood tree. They leaned out, one on either side. And Minnie and her mother were no longer swimming but standing on the grass. The smaller one she recognised as her friend and the larger one she knew was his father. He had some grey in his bearded chin and looked like an older, bigger, shaggier version of his son.

Minnie and her mother were holding bunches of wild onion in their hands. As they stood in a blaze of sunlight, the two forest beings beckoned to them with their massive hands. Minnie and her mom looked at each other, then slowly walked towards them. They stopped a few feet away, looking up at the two giants, and laid the onions on the ground. They turned, walked away, and when they looked back the onions and the Sasquatches had gone. Sitting on the emerald-green moss by the redwood was a large lump of quartz glinting in the sun.

KAAYII

Chapter Five

As the shot from the killing stick echoed through the forest, Kaayii crouched amongst the ferns near the redwood tree. He watched the man and wondered if he was the source of the strange energy Kaayii had sensed. The man was standing, staring straight ahead, his killing stick held across his chest. Between Kaayii and the man were more giant redwoods, pines, bushes, ferns, tangled fallen branches, a small gully and criss-crossing game trails, so Kaayii felt well concealed.

Kaayii crept closer, heading for the gully, and as he did so he became aware of a deep humming. It was a *very* deep hum. A hum so deep that only whales, elephants, lions, tigers and Sasquatches can produce it – a hum used to communicate, to stupefy or to terrify. Kaayii realised that this hum had silenced the forest all around.

141

Kaayii searched the high trees for movement, but the leafy canopy was still. The understory where feeding birds and bugs would flit about was devoid of activity, and at ground level Kaayii could neither see nor sense movement at all. The forest had stopped. As far as he could see and hear, not a creature was stirring, not even a louse.

The man stood, mesmerised, gazing at a tree. Kaayii could see where the bark had been blasted away, exposing the flesh of the trunk. He crawled on his hands and knees along the gully, pushing through bracken and branches until, peering through the foliage he found the source of the humming. About a pinecone's throw away from the tree, standing inside a large bush and looking directly at the man, was the biggest Sasquatch Kaayii had ever seen.

This Sasquatch was head and shoulders taller than Kaayii's father. His hair was long and grey, covering his whole body apart from his dark-grey nose and cheeks. His chest was twice as wide and deep as Kaayii's. His shoulder muscles were the size of the largest puffball mushrooms. The Sasquatch breathed in deeply and, still producing the low hum, pursed his lips and whistled. Kaayii knew this was what had stunned the man to paralysis and had allowed this giant being to move away from the man's line of sight to a safer distance. Kaayii stood transfixed as the immense grey Sasquatch bent his knees slightly and began to back away from the bush. Then, still humming, he slowly turned and looked directly at Kaayii.

The anger in his black eyes took Kaayii's breath away. Kaayii glanced over at the man, his red hat still just visible through the tangle of underbrush. The humming stopped – the man bolted, sprinting away through the trees.

Stealthily, Kaayii moved towards the tree the man had blasted with the killing stick and had a clear view back to where the man had been standing. There was no sign of the human; he had had the good sense to keep running.

In no time at all, and without making a sound, the grey Sasquatch was standing next to Kaayii, towering over him.

Pointing down the mountain and using mind-speak alone, the Grey told Kaayii: *Go. Go away!*

Kaayii looked up at the Grey, at the twisted, wrinkled skin above the thick brow shading his eyes, at the dense grey and white hair on his massive head and chin, and realised how old he was – much older than his father, but also much bigger.

For the first time since his clan had moved away to the island Kaayii spoke. Using the ancient rich and complex Sasquatch language reserved for important declarations, he uttered words which meant, 'I am guardian of the mountain'.

The Grey prodded a huge black finger at Kaayii's chest. This Sasquatch's hand was bigger than Kaayii's foot. In a voice so deep Kaayii's own chest vibrated with the resonance, the Grey chose words – rhythmic and blunt words – which carried the meaning, 'I am staying here on this mountain'.

Kaayii looked up into his eyes and sensed something more than simple anger. He lifted his hand and placed it on the old Sasquatch's chest, as the Grey swung his hand at Kaayii's head.

When Kaayii woke up, the first sensation he felt was a throbbing pain in his head. He lay on the ground among the ferns, gazing up at treetops swaying in the wind. Shakily he tried to stand. His head ached and his fingers found blood. The Grey was gone, but Kaayii could see where he had crashed through the brush, shoving and breaking everything in his path.

Something on the ground caught his eye, gleaming in the sunlight, half hidden by ferns. Kaayii bent to investigate, and blood dribbled on to a fern from a cut on his head. Reaching down, he lifted up the very thing he had travelled across the desolate, blackened forest to retrieve.

Kaayii held in his hand the only object his father valued: a lump of crystal quartz encased in a web of twisted roots. It was stained with Kaayii's blood – the Grey had struck him on the head with the piece of quartz and, in his rage, he had dropped it among the ferns.

Holding the quartz in one hand, Kaayii followed the wide path of devastation through the underbrush. Slim pines had been shoved over, limbs snapped, bushes and ferns had been grabbed and yanked out of the earth. He could still hear the sound of breaking trees. They cracked and crashed, and the sound seemed to rend the forest asunder – gone was the balanced calm, gone was the simple throb of life energy.

Kaayii caught up with the Grey but kept a safe distance of two throws from him. A dog's bark not far away stopped Kaayii in his tracks. Soon he heard panting and a hurrying patter of footsteps. The smelly yellow dog jumped up at Kaayii, apparently delighted to see him. He lifted the squirming dog in his arms.

The Grey looked back at Kaayii and the dog. Kaayii put the dog down. Seeing the Grey, the dog froze, flopped to the ground and lay on his back, trembling from head to foot. Kaayii nudged it with his toe. It jumped up, running quickly away into the trees. The Grey ploughed on through the underbrush, deeper into the forest.

Kaayii heard buzzing and began to salivate. Leaving the quartz in the grass beneath an oak with a deep hollow in its trunk, Kaayii reached to the lower branches and pulled himself up, stretching a long arm inside. Bees buzzed about his head as he pulled out a chunk of dripping honeycomb and swallowed most of it, before he remembered to thank the bees.

He wiped the wound on his still throbbing head with the back of his hairy hand, and then liberally smeared honey across the gaping red cut.

He sat in the tree, looking through the branches nervously, expecting the Grey to come crashing back towards him at any moment. He wondered at the rage of the Grey, and where he had come from. This was the unfriendliest Sasquatch he had ever met.

Dropping silently from the oak tree, he picked up the quartz again and studied it closely, wiping away his blood. The crystal was knobbly and a pinkish yellow, some flat surfaces had sharp corners that gleamed smoothly. Roots had curled around it underground, making a useful handle by which to carry it.

A sudden, deafening howl shook Kaayii to the core. Its shockwave threw him backwards. The air seemed to shimmer, and the sunlight seemed more brilliant. A pulse rippled through every root, through the billions of microscopic fungal threads linking every living plant and creature.

The blue sky glowed between the treetops. Kaayii rolled on to his side and slowly got to his feet, taking several deep breaths to settle himself. His head screamed and his ears rang.

He walked stealthily towards the source of the howl and, as he suspected, the Grey was standing back at the pine where Kaayii had found the lump of quartz.

The Grey was searching among the ferns, pushing them aside with his great hands. Grabbing the pine tree that the man had shot with the killing stick, he shook it violently. Pine needles rained down on the Grey. He brushed them off his head angrily. Kaayii hid behind a mulberry bush, his heart racing.

The Grey sat down amongst the ferns, head and shoulders visible, and Kaayii moved quickly to a broad fir tree and sat hidden by the low, feathered boughs. His head still ached; he lay down on the dense carpet of dry pine needles and closed his eyes.

An eagle's scream pierced the stillness and roused Kaayii from his nap. He sat up, rubbed his head and crawled out from under the tree. He saw no sign of the Grey, just a wide patch of flattened ferns.

Through the canopy he caught a fleeting glimpse of a familiar silhouette. Wheeling on the warm currents high above was the resident golden eagle holding a large pink salmon in its bright yellow talons. The eagle made a lazy circle, spiralling lower and lower.

Kaayii ran, trying to keep track of it. Flapping its vast arching wings to stall its flight, the eagle landed on the top of a nearby pine. Kaayii leapt over fallen trunks and bounded over bushes. He struggled to find the eagle's pine amongst so many towering trees.

Snap! Nearly halfway up a smooth straight pine, the Grey was climbing, up and up.

The Grey was under the eagle's nest in moments. Ripping apart the nest, flinging great handfuls of branches and twigs away, he grabbed hold of the salmon.

Its wings askew, the eagle tumbled off the nest. Kaayii expected it to hit the ground but somehow it twisted and flapped at the last moment and, in the blink of an eye, swooped away through the trees, screeching its wretched call.

A steady distant droning took his attention away from the bird. Between the trees he caught sight of a plane as it buzzed past like a giant yellow seagull.

The wind had picked up, the mountain pines' high tops knocked together, needles rustling, as the Grey dropped from the lowest branch still munching on the salmon. He pulled its tail out of his mouth and flung it away.

Kaayii's head was aching and he thought he might have to lie down again and wait for the pain to pass, but the Grey was on the move and Kaayii knew that if he started to head towards the humans, Kaayii would have to do something to stop him.

The Grey paralleled the shore for a while, keeping among the denser conifers. Kaayii saw him stop to sniff the air and wondered if the Grey had ever seen the sea before, whether its salty freshness was new to him.

The yellow plane flew past again, lower this time, then climbed and turned and Kaayii lost sight of it.

Rain began to fall as Kaayii watched the Grey standing still among the firs, gazing across the water to the island, now shrouded in a wispy cloud. For a moment he thought the Grey might climb down to the sea and swim away, which would solve the young Sasquatch's problem, but

Kaayii wasn't surprised that without knowledge of the tides and the currents in this passage of water, the Grey turned and climbed back up the slope.

The rain lashed down in a sudden squall blasted inland on strong winds, as the Grey cut up the grassy slope near the Aspen Grove. His head was as high as the tallest branches on the elegant slim white trunks. Kaayii followed at a safe distance.

Planting his massive feet before the Giant X , the Grey studied the biggest structure Kaayii had made in the forest – perfectly symmetrical broken-off tree trunks, stripped of their bark and heaved into place to mark a junction of energy under the ground. The Grey walked up to it, lifted one of the tree trunks and pulled it away collapsing the X. Kaayii stood, mouth agape, stunned.

The Grey, like all Sasquatches, knew that where there was one structure there would be others. So he walked straight up the hill through the underbrush to the next Big X, which he simply pushed until it broke free of the trees it was wedged in and fell to the forest floor. Next he found a 'tripod' structure, a distinctive branch that had grown three separate limbs like a three-pronged fork. It had been stuck in the ground and leant against a tree. The Grey shoved it over.

The young Sasquatch feared what this angry being might do next. Inevitably the Grey strolled back down the slope and, spotting the tumble of piled up pine boughs, went over to investigate Kaayii's special Watcher's Place.

The Grey eased his immense frame into the nest of deep moss, grass and ferns. With a clear view of the game trail winding its way down the slope and of the islands of the bay beyond the tops of the pines, the Grey settled in, pulled up some ferns and placed them over his head to keep the rain off.

Kaayii thought about the time he'd first seen the girl and the boy from this place. If humans came close to the Grey or if the Grey went too close to humans, it would not end well. He hoped the sighting of the man with the killing stick had not made the Grey curious. The Grey was too dangerous to leave unattended for long, and too big and too strong for Kaayii to control on his own, so Kaayii ran, clutching the quartz by its root handle, straight up through the forest, heading for the cave. He needed help.

Chapter Six

Huff and Mook were sheltering from the heavy rainfall under a conifer near the pond when they sensed Kaayii's presence. Pushing through the branches they peered at the shaded depths of the dripping forest, and presently Kaayii emerged. They ran to him. He bent to greet them and they leapt at his head to lick the honey on his wound.

The pond's surface danced under the deluge as the young Sasquatch knelt to drink. Standing in the water near the swaying brown heads of the cattails, he grasped one by its thick lower stalk and pulled it out, biting the roots and peeling back the young green leaves. There was a clear jelly under the leaves and, wiping it up with a finger, he smeared it across the cut on his head. Then he ate the white stalk and the green leaves, crunching them with his square teeth.

Willows grew near the pond, their branches arching under the weight of plentiful long leaves. Kaayii searched at the base and pulled up young shoots, thin and flexible. He could bite the wider ends and split them down the middle without them breaking. He carried a handful as he climbed the path between the grey boulders that led up to High Ridge. The wolves trotted along behind him.

On the edge of the high meadow, he placed the quartz and the willow switches in the grass and climbed his favourite pine tree. On the edge of the ridge, it offered a commanding view down the mountain to the bay and from its heights he could view the long dark island, over which clouds had gathered. Waves were capping white on the water. The wind came straight across the bay and swayed the young Sasquatch on his perch.

Somewhere on that curve of hills across the bay his clan was hunting, gathering, eating and laughing together. Exposed to the rain and wind Kaayii felt a bite of loneliness. Concentrating his mind on his father and mother, he waited, hoping for some guidance. After a while he climbed down the tree, dropping softly to the forest floor.

Back in the cave, he sat listening to the rain crashing and splashing on the boulders outside. The wolves had stashed some meat from a deer whose time had come to pass. They fed on it, leaving some for Kaayii, but he didn't eat. A plan was forming in his mind.

He lifted the quartz, studying the bloodstained roots. He wound and tightened split willow strips to fashion a binding around the handle.

While the wolves slept, Kaayii wove together more thin shoots of bendy willow whips. He had learnt from his father and uncle how to make twisted shapes and figures for his young sister to play with. He split the willow and bent small loops for a head, attaching a shorter length for the arms. He twisted the willow around to form a body and legs. Then, pulling some straggly bits of moss from the wolves' bed, he threaded the moss piece by piece through loops, then tightened the loops to hold the 'hair' in place. He studied the doll in the black palm of his hand. It was about the size of his thumb.

Pre-dawn, the storm had passed, the rainfall had ceased, and a timid-looking crescent moon grinned between passing clouds. They crossed the meadow and drank briefly at the pond.

Kaayii made three short whistling peeps and soon the crow cawed in greeting, alighting on a nearby branch to await instructions. Kaayii held the lump of quartz by its root handle and the small willow-twist figure in the other hand. He stood before the crow and told it by thought alone to watch the grey Sasquatch. With a frantic flapping of black wings that flashed silver in the moonlight, the crow flew away into the forest.

Avoiding the slippery, moss-covered rocks by the stream, Kaayii and the wolves hurried along game trails, scattering rats, mice and squirrels. In the grove of ancient cedars, twisted arbutus, shaggy hemlocks and gnarly oaks which dripped with grey lichen and spongy green moss, Kaayii paused at what he now thought of as the 'hukkoobay' bush, grazing briefly on the purple berries and sharing some with the wolves.

Standing by the road the trio sniffed the sea breeze. The tide was high. The wolves ran across the road and down to the rocks, jumping into the sea and splashing about in the shallows. A gruff bark sounded from near one of the small islands. Staring into the dark, Kaayii saw moonlight sparking briefly in a splash. With icy-cold water washing at his knees, he made a low guttural answering bark. He scanned the water. It was still;

the usual flock of seagulls floated together near the closer of the two small islands. He barked again.

Seagulls fluttered wings and lifted from the surface, as the head of a seal appeared among them. The smooth black head glided towards the shore, looking like an earless dog, with large, round, glassy, black eyes. The seal barked once at Kaayii. The wolves stopped what they were doing and, gazing back at their sea-cousin, barked short tetchy woofs. Kaayii told them to be quiet, glancing up at the cabins.

Picking up the quartz and the small, twisted willow figure, he walked to the jetty, remembering that night when he had stood in the shadows and watched as every member of his clan ran and jumped off the end, swimming away from the mountain, away from the forest, and away from Kaayii.

He scanned the dark cabins and, sensing no movement, he lowered himself into the water and waded out to the dinghies tied to the jetty. Reaching over the side of a dinghy, he carefully placed the quartz on the seatboard, positioning the root to point away from the mountain, directly at the island. He tucked the small willow figure beneath it.

At that moment a light went on in the nearest cabin, one of the two up on the rise, casting a weak yellow beam across the grass. Kaayii ducked down behind the dinghy. Hugging one of the jetty posts he watched as the man who had fired the killing stick in the forest came out. He stood on the deck, looking down at the jetty. Kaayii could see the man clearly but he knew humans had poor eyesight at night, even with a partial moon. The wolves stood stock-still in the shadows down on the shore watching the man. The seal floated, watching the man. Kaayii watched the man. The man shifted to the edge of the deck, peering into the darkness. He turned, went back inside the cabin, and the light flicked off.

The seal's head appeared by Kaayii's side. The sleek black creature nudged Kaayii's leg with his nose. With a twist and a flick of its tail it turned and dived under the water. Kaayii dived under with barely a splash and swam in the darkness as far as his breath would allow. He floated in the dark, gazing up through the surface at the tremulous distant moon, as the seal danced and dived around him. Kaayii followed the sleek creature, swimming out and diving down deeper as the seal shot by, swung round, and passed him again and again.

Kaayii stood chest deep in the gentle waves and let his hands hang loose. He breathed in deeply and on the exhalation imagined threads of energy emitting from his fingers. A fish brushed his arm and with a whoosh Kaayii grasped it in one vast hand and heaved it over to the seal, who caught it in his gaping jaws and munched it down greedily.

The dull grey light of dawn began to trace the tops of the mountain as Kaayii waded out of the water. The Sasquatch and the wolves hurried back through the grove, running up the well-trodden game trail that weaved through the giant ferns and ancient twisted trees, cutting up to and over the main hiking trail, and up into the forest.

As they approached the Watcher's Place they slowed, treading with extra care, listening for the Grey. Kaayii called for the crow with his special three-peep whistle. He called again – nothing.

Even in the weak dawn light Kaayii could see there was a big Sasquatch-sized impression in the moss of his nest at the Watcher's Place. In the middle of it lay the broken body of the crow, his eyes glazed, his claws closed like two big, dead spiders.

The young Sasquatch swayed, his head throbbed and his world spun. His legs gave way. Squatting on the ground, his arms hugging the trunk of a tree, he rested his forehead on the mottled bark. Huff and Mook sniffed the body of the crow.

Kaayii dug in the ground with a stick and gently placed the crow in the shallow grave, covering the bird with earth and leaves. He pressed it firm with his hands, humming as he did so, thanking the bird for his friendship. The wolves stood either side of him, their heads gently pressed against his knees.

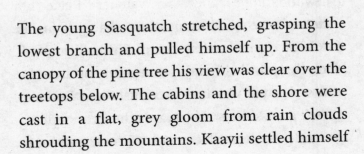

The young Sasquatch stretched, grasping the lowest branch and pulled himself up. From the canopy of the pine tree his view was clear over the treetops below. The cabins and the shore were cast in a flat, grey gloom from rain clouds shrouding the mountains. Kaayii settled himself in the fork of a stout upper branch, and wondered where the Grey was. Kaayii knew that as long as he could see the humans' cabins, he would know the Grey was not down there. He hoped the Grey was far away up the mountain.

Dozing with his arms tight around the trunk, he was soothed by the gentle sway of the tree until, sensing activity on the shore, his eyes snapped open. It was early for humans to be out of their structures but he could see the man again, standing on the grass looking down at the stretch of muddy beach the receding tide had revealed: the man who'd fired the killing stick.

This time the man climbed down the boulders on to the shore. Kaayii was sure he hadn't left any prints in the gritty sand earlier, but he was also sure there would be wolf prints where they'd frolicked, hunting for worms by the high-tide driftwood.

Indeed, the man soon found the wolf prints and bent over to study them. He held a small black thing in his hand, pointing it towards the prints. Kaayii watched anxiously as the man walked across the sand towards the jetty stepping over tide pools and seaweed. Climbing up onto the jetty he walked to the end and looked out. The bay beyond the small islands was calm: seagulls floated in flocks and wading birds searched the mud.

The man climbed down from the jetty into the shallow water and onto the beach. He waded over to the blue dinghy floating inches above the mud. Reaching down he lifted the quartz. He kept glancing up at the cabins. Kaayii gripped a tree branch for support, stretching to watch the man picking up the twisted-willow doll with the moss hair. The man studied both objects very carefully, now and then looking up warily at the cabins.

Turning the quartz in his hand he must have seen the blood on the underside, as he recoiled slightly, and to Kaayii's relief, replaced the lump of quartz exactly as he found it. Then he stepped away from the dinghy, with the doll. Hissing angrily Kaayii broke the branch he was holding. *CRACK!*

The man looked up. Scanning the forested slopes from left to right, he sought the source of the noise. Kaayii barked out a short but powerfully loud and deep, 'Naarghh!'

For a moment, the man hesitated, a fearful

expression on his face; it looked like he was about to replace the doll. Then he waded away from the small boats, across the strip of grey sand still holding the small doll in one hand. Kaayii watched as he climbed back up, his mouth fixed in a tight smile, and walked quickly back up to his cabin.

Kaayii climbed down the pine and wandered away, kicking a rotten log, which rolled down the game trail knocking into a conifer. Beneath the fir's lowest feathery boughs, Kaayii noticed a cluster of mushrooms growing in overlapping wavy plates of creamy orange. This was one of Kaayii's favourites. He pulled handfuls of the soft and fleshy fungus and, lying on his back, dropped chunks into his mouth. He buried his face in the crown of a clump of ferns to suck up the water that pooled there to wash down his breakfast. Feeling slightly better, he climbed the tree again.

MINNIE

Chapter Seven

Minnie woke early. The rain had stopped and she could hear no activity. Dan must still be in bed, she reckoned. As she lay gazing at the ceiling, she thought of her Bigfoot friend. Then she remembered her dream, of swimming through the forest with her mother, of seeing the two Bigfoots. She wondered what it meant and guessed that she had the dream because she was worried.

Dressing quickly, she was soon out on the deck. She rubbed her sleepy eyes, scratched her head, looked up at Billy's cabin and over at cabin number four – nobody about. She walked to the end of the deck and gazed across the glassy black water. The sun was just topping the mountain behind her, so Bigfoot Island was bathed in an early morning glow but the cabins and the water sat in a grey, flat, pre-dawn shade.

She went back inside and looked at the clock on the wall above the fridge. It was only half past five.

'Huh, that's why everything looks weird. What am I doing up so early?' she said to herself, filling a glass and drinking the cool water.

Usually, she'd be awakened by Dan making his coffee. It was such a small cabin and the walls so thin that the sound of the kettle boiling on the other side of the wall, inches from her head, was like a swarm of angry hornets.

She decided to wander down to the shore and paddle in the shallows and splash her face with seawater. So, barefoot in her green pjs, she trotted down the deck steps and down the grassy slope.

The tide was going out. Minnie hoisted up the baggy green pyjama legs, stepping out on to the grey mud and stood in a rock pool in shin-high cold water.

Along the shoreline a black oystercatcher paced patiently. Its jet-black wings neatly folded, it strode on long pinkish legs, back and forth, scrutinising the mud.

'Morning, birdie. Any luck?' It had vivid orange eyes and a long bright-red beak for probing among the rocks for limpets, mussels and worms.

Beyond the bird's feet, where pieces of seaweed and driftwood marked the high-tide mark, Minnie thought she could see footprints, dozens of them.

She peered down, 'Wolf. Hmm … interesting.' She bent to study them. 'One. Or two wolves. And a person, in trainers. Huh!'

Minnie climbed on to the jetty, remembering the incredible gift her Bigfoot friend had left, weeks ago now, of a seafood 'platter', laid out in a circle on the boards. He'd caught salmon and sea trout and gathered up sea kelp, laying it out with mussels, limpets, and oysters on the jetty. Though the seagulls had demolished some of it, there had been enough fresh food to feed the four of them for supper that evening.

She walked along to the end of the boards and was about to sit and dangle her legs, when something caught her eye in one of the dinghies resting on the mud. She climbed down and realised what it was. Sitting on the painted seatboard of the blue dinghy was a lump of pink quartz about the size of a pineapple. It was enclosed in a web of tree roots that looked like they had naturally grown around the crystal, while it had been waiting under ground for thousands of years. The ends of the root were secured with a neat willow knot. The stoutest bit of root sticking out was about eight inches long, also wrapped with split willow, and made a perfect handle.

It seemed to have been positioned carefully, with the long root directly in line with the keel, pointing forward to the bow of the dinghy, towards Bigfoot Island. That morning's dream returned to her mind in an instant – the dream of the two Bigfoots leaving her and her mother a piece of quartz, and it sent a shiver up her spine.

Holding it aloft in both hands, and looking up at the mountain, she danced a gleeful little jig – dancing like no one was watching her, except, she suspected, one giant, hairy Sasquatch.

She studied the piece of quartz crystal, examining the smooth bumps and curves and only then did she realise that the roots on the underside were stained with a dried smear of darkened blood. She gasped and nearly dropped it. She hurried off the grey gritty mud, clambering up the bank to the grass, and ran with the quartz up the grassy slope. She needed Dan to see it immediately.

'You're right, Min. Two wolves, I reckon. This will unsettle our guests even more! Should we brush them away?'

'No, look, Dan. Trainer prints, on the beach. Alex has already seen 'em!'

'Oh, yeah. Right.'

'They're leaving anyway, soon as Sam gets here, so...'

'Yeah, OK.'

'Well, *they* didn't leave the quartz. The wolves, I mean. There were no footprints by the dingy.'

'No, right...' said Dan, looking up at the mountain. 'So it can't have been left by Alex. Unless he did it while the tide was in, right?'

'Oh. Yeah. He could have. But I don't think it was Alex. I know it wasn't Alex. It was my Sasquatch. He needs help.'

'Who?'

'My Sasquatch. It's a sign.'

'It's a gift, probably. Like the seafood was.'

'It's a sign.'

'Gift.'

'Sign. He's injured. And needs help.'

169

'Well, I need coffee.' With that Dan started up the slope. 'And I'm going to ask Alex if he knows anything about the quartz.'

'Well, I need to show Billy.' She climbed up to the grassy bank and ran up the slope holding the quartz by its handle.

'Minnie, wait. Billy doesn't know there is still at least one Bigfoot on the mountain.'

'Oh yeah.'

'You gonna tell him?'

'Hmm… I dunno.'

'So, Minnie, let me get this straight. I'm the only person who didn't know there was a Bigfoot right here, on our mountain?'

'Yeah, sorry, Billy-Bug. I didn't think you could handle it. And it's not our mountain.'

'Well, I *can* handle it, see!' Billy was demolishing a bowl of oatmeal.

'OK, OK, keep your pants on!'

Minnie settled on the bench and pushed the quartz across the table, a little closer to Billy.

'So what do you think it means?' asked Minnie,

as Connie came out to the deck with a jug of orange juice.

'It don't mean nothin' at all,' spluttered Billy. 'It's just a gift.'

'Please don't talk with your mouth full of oats, Billy.'

Minnie held the quartz in her hands. 'That's what Dan thinks.'

'A very weird kind of gift,' said Connie. 'I mean, with blood on it.' Minnie lifted the quartz.

'A gift from my BFF.'

Billy looked at Minnie. 'Excuse me, from who? Your what?'

'My BFF.'

Billy put his hands on his hips and said, 'How dare you?'

Minnie answered, 'It means Big Footed Friend, silly.'

'Oh, that's OK then.'

'Look, a hummingbird!' said Connie. 'I haven't seen one here all summer.'

The thumb-sized bird's head, throat and wings were a reddish-brown, its whirring wings were a blur. It stuck its long black beak into a honeysuckle flower, probing for nectar.

'Your mom loved these,' said Connie. 'It's called a Rufus Hummingbird.'

'Rufus?' queried Billy.

'It means reddish-brown.'

'That would be a good name for my Sasquatch,' said Minnie. 'Rufus. I've been trying to think of a name for him.'

'Well, what about Roy?' offered Billy. 'It means king but *also* means red. And it's the five hundred and forty-second most popular name in North America.'

They were all three transfixed by the tiny hovering bird, the speed of its wings playing a constant hum to accompany its dance from flower to flower.

'It's also your father's name, Billy,' said Minnie gently.

'Well,' said Connie, 'sightings are equally rare.'

Connie turned to Minnie. 'I think Rufus is an excellent name for a Bigfoot. Is his fur red?'

'Hair not fur. Yes, I think so. I only saw him that one night with you all.'

'He smelt super funky,' said Billy. 'Eww...'

'Lemonade, Dan?' called Connie to Dan who was coming up the track.

Billy stood up. 'Stinkum!'

'Hello to you too, Billy.' Dan trod the five wooden steps and leant against the deck rail. Musto bustled over to join him and Dan pulled the dog's ear affectionately.

'Well, Alex swears he didn't leave the quartz. But he was on the beach and he saw the wolf tracks. He's real twitchy. Can't wait to get outta here.'

Dan lifted the quartz and examined it closely. 'What do you think, Connie?'

'Oh, amazing, beautiful.'

'Or Moss!' declared Billy. 'That's a good name.'

Minnie looked at him. 'Moss is better than Stinkum. But not as good as Rufus.'

'Oh, a hummingbird,' Dan said, spotting the tiny bird moving along the white flowers.

'In Native American culture,' said Connie, 'when a hummingbird crosses your path it signifies joy and playfulness, and is a reminder of the lightness of being, and the lifting away of negativity.'

Minnie looked at Billy smiling. 'Ya hear that Billy-Bug? Lifting away negativity.'

'So, this was left in the dinghy by a Bigfoot.

Sorry, your Bigfoot.' Dan studied the quartz turning it in his hand. 'How about that.' He sounded doubtful.

Minnie smiled at Dan. 'I prefer Sasquatch.'

'His name is Moss,' said Billy. 'I thought of it.'

'He has a name now?' said Dan. 'When's he moving in?'

'Not Moss, maybe Rufus. I haven't decided yet,' Minnie said.

'You haven't decided when he's moving in?'

'No, I haven't decided if that's his name!'

'They must have names for each other,' said Connie. 'If they're as smart as you say, Minnie?'

'Right.'

'It would be like him thinking of a name for you,' said Connie. 'Like whatever Sasquatch is for curly!'

They laughed.

'I would like that,' said Minnie. 'I wonder what that is!'

Dan put the quartz on the table and pulled up a chair. 'Minnie, you don't think Marshal put this in the dinghy? I couldn't ask him; he was still sleeping.'

'Oh please,' snorted Minnie with derision.

'Where would he have got this? All he knows is how to look at a phone. Besides, it has blood on it.'

'So, it's a gift…'

'No, it's more than that,' said Minnie, now standing up, the better to address the three most important and, in her mind, most wonderful humans on the planet with the sombre note the moment required. She announced, 'It's a sign. Well, more of a message.'

'What does an eagle mean then?' Billy was gazing up into the sky. High above them soaring on the summer thermals was the distinctive silhouette of an eagle.

'Billy, I'm saying something!'

'Your eagle's back, Min,' said Dan, shading his eyes from the sun.

'An eagle totem,' said Connie. 'It can soar to great heights but is also grounded, strongly connected to the earth. Eagle totem means accepting life's challenges with great courage, confidence and determination. That's you for sure, Minnie!'

'OK. Thank you. Now please, listen. I know what this means,' she said pointing up at the eagle, 'now that Connie has explained it. And I know what this means,' she said, pointing at the quartz. 'And I know where we have to go.'

Dan looked at Minnie with mounting trepidation. 'What do you have in mind now?'

'He helped me. In the forest when I fell. Now we have to help him.'

'And...?'

'And I think this is a message for the others, over there. I think he is injured and needs their help.'

'Interesting theory,' said Billy.

'If he's well enough to bring this lump of quartz down here, why doesn't he swim over to the island?' asked Dan.

'Maybe he can't swim?' suggested Billy.

'Something is keeping him here. He wants *us* to go. That's why he left it in the boat.'

'Well, that ain't gonna happen,' said Dan, and he downed his drink, put the glass on the table and headed for the steps.

Minnie hurried after him. 'We'll leave the crystal there for them to find! They'll understand!'

'No.'

'We've got to do it today, Dad! When Sam gets back. He'll take us over there. We'll be back in no time! When's he due?'

'He's taking them to Vardy! They have a flight to catch!'

In their cabin, Minnie stood by the door, twisting a curl of hair anxiously round and round a finger. Dan was talking on his phone.

'Sure, OK, I'll let them know… Yes. Thanks, Sam, bye.'

He put the phone on the table and looked at Minnie.

'Sam has mechanical issues on the boat. He can't make it till later today at best.'

Minnie stepped closer.

'Dad, you have to trust me.'

Moving to the open door he stepped out and looked at the weather. It was clear and bright above the big island across the bay.

'Canoe, Dad.'

'It's too dangerous.'

'Please. We have to accept the challenge with great courage, confidence and determination. You know, like an eagle?'

Minnie and Billy waited on the jetty as Dan and

Connie carried the canoe down the grassy slope, from its place under a green tarpaulin behind cabin number one.

Alex, Cristy and Marshal were sitting on their deck with their luggage neatly stacked and ready.

As they got to the jetty with the canoe, Connie asked Dan, 'Can't you wait for Sam to come back, and he can take you there?'

'No, we have to do it now,' said Minnie, showing Connie the underside of the quartz again. 'There is blood. He is injured. We have to go.' She carefully lowered the quartz into her small red backpack, slipped her thin measuring stick in, and zipped it up.

Dan handed her a lifejacket, which she dropped into the canoe and they lowered it onto the water.

Connie put a hand on Dan's arm. 'Minnie's instincts were right before, and you listened to her. You moved the cabin. But this is different. That's their island, over there.'

'And I'm listening to her again. I'm trusting her again, and it's important to her, so...' He pulled Minnie to his side and hugged her, and she smiled up at him. 'It'll be fine. I want to leave now while the tide is slack.'

He lobbed two single-length wooden paddles into the canoe. 'We'll see you later.'

'Please be careful,' said Connie, and she kissed Minnie on the top of her head.

'We can't persuade you to stay a little longer?' called Dan to the Ashton-Kitto family, who were watching from their deck with interest.

'We're expecting Sam to be here so no,' called Alex. 'Thanks.'

Cristy and Marshal started wandering down from the cabin.

'Where ya going?' asked Cristy.

'Just across the bay,' replied Dan.

Alex walked down the deck steps. 'Across the bay? Why? Nothin' over there.'

'Just a little expedition,' said Minnie.

'Will you be back before we leave?' asked Cristy.

'Oh yes,' said Dan. 'Sam won't be here till late afternoon, at best, so...'

'This afternoon?' Alex was aghast.

'Oh, yeah, sorry, he just called me. Had a problem with the boat. Drive-chain ... engine ... something... He'll be leaving soon, probably. Meant to tell you.'

'Great!' Alex's sarcasm was blunt to the point of rudeness.

'I'm sorry you don't like it here, Alex,' said Dan. 'Sorry you're so disappointed you can't leave soon enough!'

Cristy put a restraining hand on Alex's arm. Alex glanced down at the dinghy, seeing that the crystal was no longer there.

'Don't worry about bears while we're gone,' said Minnie. 'Connie and Billy will protect you.'

This made Marshal laugh. Alex approached the canoe, frowning, and said, 'Listen, I don't know what kind of wildlife you're comfortable with here. Wolves, bears, cougars I can handle, same as the next guy, but...'

'But?' asked Dan as he hoisted his backpack into the canoe.

'If you're going over there you should maybe know something.'

'Alex...' began Cristy.

'You might be interested to know that we heard a howl over there. Yeah, a howl. Much like the one yesterday. A godawful, freaky, monster howl from hell. We also found footprints, like yay big.' Alex held his hands apart. 'And you might care to know that it was *not* a bear we saw up here in your woods!'

They all stared at the pompous man.

'What was it?' asked Dan casually.

'It was…'

'Dad, don't,' said Marshal.

'I don't know what it was, but it was not a bear. It was grey, huge, hairy. I saw its arm, and … and … and then …then … and it looked right at me, and…' Tears welled in his eyes and Cristy put an arm round his shoulders.

'It's OK, Alex,' said Dan, 'we know about them. Let's go, Minnie.' He climbed into the canoe and pulled his life jacket on, as Connie and Billy held the ropes at either end. It wobbled on the water as he took Minnie's hand and she climbed down, taking a seat in the front, pulling on her life jacket.

They pushed off.

'See you later!'

Connie waved. 'Sure you got enough water?'

'Yeah, yeah, bye, Connie. See ya, Billy-Boy!'

'So when *exactly* did Sam say he'd be back?' called Alex.

'Afternoon some time,' called Dan. 'Try to

relax! Go swimming! Go fishing! Try not to shoot anything!'

As Minnie and Dan paddled between the small, wooded islands, little waves splashed on the pointed, up-turned prow of the canoe and Minnie's hair was soon damp.

Dan glanced back over his shoulder at the cove.

'He really needs to learn to relax.'

'I know,' said Minnie, unzipping her backpack and pulling out a water bottle.

Dan gestured at the larger of the small islands as they edged past. 'This island would be a good place for a swimming platform, don't ya think?'

A few large boulders were grouped together around the base and the island was topped with a couple of tall pines, some smaller windswept pines, a short sea-oak and some scrubby grass.

'Yeah,' said Minnie. 'Maybe after we finish the new cabin.'

Dan pulled steadily on his paddle. 'It's good to be on the water.'

Each had a single cross-board bench to sit and

paddle from. Minnie braced her feet on the slats in the bottom of the open canoe. The steady, easy, rhythmic paddling was soothing. She looked back at Bigfoot Mountain. The water was calm with a gently heaving swell that the canoe rode easily.

'How long should it take to get over there?' asked Minnie, as seagulls called from high above.

'Forty minutes or so, I guess.'

Without a sound, a seal's head appeared near the canoe – sleek, shiny and black. It gazed at Minnie, then Dan.

Minnie was delighted. 'Hi there!'

'Hi, seal!' said Dan as, with a curl of its back, it dived down and away. 'I could have sworn that seal was smiling!'

An hour later, Dan had long-since stopped chatting. The land mass had grown larger very slowly, as the minutes passed, and they could see the shoreline now, with a slim stretch of pale sand. The island was higher and longer than it seemed from Cabin Cove. The green hills towered above them, completely covered by ancient pines and firs, just like all the land round here for miles and miles, whether islands, hills, mountains, or valleys.

The sea had become slightly rougher as they

approached the shore and the waves were choppy. Minnie was getting tired of paddling and Dan was doing most of the work.

'I'm sorry this is taking longer than I thought, Minnie,' Dan said.

'It's OK,' she said. 'We're nearly there.'

'The tide's going out and pulling us with it,' he called, as a gust of wind seemed to come out of nowhere and pulled the blue cap off his head and blew it far across the water.

'Let's head straight and we'll land down there.' He pointed with his paddle to a deep crease in the carpet of green trees.

Driftwood bobbed and rolled with the waves and on more than one occasion they had to back-paddle to get round a vast, bleached tree trunk.

'There's so many dead-heads floating here! Logs! So much flotsam!' yelled Dan.

'And just as much jetsom!' called Minnie. 'Though I'm not sure what the difference is!'

'Jetsom has been thrown off a boat and flotsam has floated away of its own accord!'

'Oh. OK. Good to know!'

They paddled hard against the current.

'We're over a sand bar!' Dan pointed, and below

the surface of the water sand was clearly visible. 'Can't be more than six feet and getting shallower!' Dan pulled hard on his paddle. It was hard work, the tide was running fast, but soon they could see the sand bar passing just a few feet beneath them. Dan tested the depth with his paddle. 'Yeah! Three feet!'

Neither Minnie nor Dan saw the floating tree until it was too late. The canoe rode up and on to the slim trunk, and a short point of broken branch punched a hole in the canoe's hull. The canoe twisted over on the tree, tossing Minnie, Dan and their gear into the water.

Dan grabbed Minnie by the back of her life jacket and the canoe rope with the other hand.

'You OK?' Dan yelled.

'Yeah! My backpack!'

'I'll get it!' Dan pushed the canoe towards the shore, never letting go of Minnie. They were able to pull the half-swamped canoe as they waded through shallower water. Dan lobbed his backpack towards the shore and waded out after Minnie's red one, but it bobbed away out of his reach.

Minnie pulled the canoe until it ran aground

on the beach. She dragged Dan's backpack up on to the shore, then watched horrified as her backpack seemed to float further away from Dan with every passing moment.

Standing waist high in the surf, Dan unfastened his life jacket and hurled it up on to the sand. He ran along in the shallows towards the red backpack, which kept disappearing between the waves.

'No, Dad!' Minnie called running after him. 'It's too rough!'

Dan ran into the waves and swam out through churning surf. The wind blasted white spray off the tops of the waves and Minnie put her hands to her mouth and called again as loudly as she was able.

'Dan! Leave it! Come back!'

Directly above her, but high, very high, was her golden eagle, flying above the rainy squall. Minnie couldn't focus on the bird in her fear. Wind whipped her hair across her face. Jumbled fragments of a dream or a memory of her mother took shape – her smile, her form as she walked away barefoot towards the sea, her eyes, her echoing laughter. They filled the girl with a golden warmth and a surging strength that made her stand and run along the beach, past scattered blue-grey boulders.

The red backpack was now in clear view. The wind at this end of the beach had lessened, and the water was less choppy. Minnie caught sight of Dan ploughing on between waves. He seemed to be getting closer and closer to her backpack.

Finally, he staggered out of the churning sea, wading through the surf breaking on the sand bar, clutching the backpack.

He flopped on to the firm sand. She embraced him, her body shaking with cold.

'Thank you!' Minnie unzipped the main compartment. She lifted out the quartz. Blood was still stuck to the roots around the crystal though some water had seeped into the backpack.

Dan lay, gasping, on the sand.

'I thought … I'd lost it … it sank … but … it suddenly … reappeared!'

A smooth black head broke the surface in the trough between two waves, curled its back and with a flick of its flippers was gone.

Chapter Eight

Dan and Minnie tipped the canoe over to drain the water out. There was an ugly rip in the bottom where the canoe had thumped into the floating tree. The wind had increased and he had to yell to be heard. 'Let's get this into the treeline!'

They carried the canoe between them, passing the high-tide mark, where the pinkish grey sand was littered with debris – seaweed, smaller rocks and pebbles, piles of sticks, tree trunks and branches.

'We'll leave it up here and find a place to get warm!'

Minnie looked back across the water in the direction of Bigfoot Mountain, but it was shrouded in cloud and she couldn't tell where the water stopped and the sky began – it was all one gloomy, grey mass.

The wind brought the first smatterings of rain. Minnie pulled her hood up. They walked into the forest a short way and crawled in under the branches of a conifer. Inside, under the low-sweeping, feathery boughs they were well sheltered from the elements.

Dan began pulling things out of his backpack, including a snap-top box with sandwiches in it, four bananas, two large bottles of water, a phone battery charger, a towel, black garbage bags and a thermos flask.

'Wow, Dan! Were you expecting us to be marooned on the island overnight?'

'No, but I thought we'd stop for a snack at least. Maybe catch a fish.'

With a triumphant smile Dan lifted a long thin black box. 'I have my ultralight collapsible Escape Travel Spinning Rod!'

Minnie thought to herself how Dan was the perfect person with whom to be stranded on an island.

'Now, we need to assess the situation, Minnie.' Dan was checking his phone. 'No service.'

'Yes, and decide where we're going to leave the crystal.'

He handed her his water bottle. 'How are you, Min? Any scratches or scrapes?'

'No, I think I'm fine.'

She unscrewed the top of the bottle and took a long slug of water.

'You did really well, Minnie. It was a little hairy when we went over that piece of driftwood but you didn't panic and we got everything back safe, right?'

Somewhere, a seal barked and they both glanced seawards.

'Ha!' said Dan. 'That's our friend, the seal.'

'We can't paddle back today, right, Dan? And Sam won't be coming in this weather? Too rough?'

'Listen, Minnie, I'm real sorry to get us in this situation. I checked the weather report and it said there was a "system" blowing in tonight. I guess it got here early. I'm sorry, but we're stuck here, for now.'

'It's OK.' Minnie held her backpack tight to her chest. 'Stuff happens to adventurers, otherwise it wouldn't be an adventure.'

Dan was still looking at his phone, moving it around, lifting it up. 'Still nothing. Connie will be worried.'

'And Billy.'

Dan looked at the dripping girl, soaked from head to toe, but still smiling bravely.

'We'll be fine here for one night, Minnie.'

Dan took her soaking wet backpack and hung it up from a short branch.

'When we don't return, Connie will call Sea Rescue, or Sam will come get us. Now, let's get dry.'

Dan's backpack was twice the size of Minnie's and seemed to be magically bottomless; more and more useful stuff kept appearing as he dug deeper – two sweaters, two shiny silver space blankets, a flashlight, spare socks, another water bottle.

'You should take off your wet bottoms and put this dry sweater on your legs.' Minnie was shivering.

'Were you a boy scout?' she asked, pulling off the drenched black leggings.

'No, why?'

'You're awfully well prepared,' she laughed.

'Ha! I always prepare for the unexpected.'

She pulled his green sweater on over her legs.

'Put this spare jacket on too.' He handed her a green windcheater.

'Why is this island uninhabited by people, Dan?' Minnie parted two boughs and looked out. They were only a few trees in and she could see to the shoreline, with the boulders strewn along the beach and the churning water beyond. The receding tide had left a wide beach of dark, wet sand.

'Well, it's real steep, right from the shore straight up, all the way around. Too steep for logging, so nobody bothered to settle here.'

The trees and the undergrowth of ferns, grasses and bushes were the same as on Bigfoot Mountain and Minnie felt somewhat comforted. The phrase 'a home away from home' passed through her mind.

'My shorts will be dry soon enough,' Dan stretched his legs out. 'We need a fire.'

'How will we start a fire?' Minnie asked and Dan delved in his backpack. He produced a small black metal rod about as long as a pencil, and a knife with a bone handle.

'Do not fret! I have this!'

'What's that?'

He handed the tools to her. 'My fire starter rod and my Cold Steel Compact Bushmaster Camp knife. Scrape one against the other and we shall have fire! Well, sparks.'

'Er, you maybe haven't noticed, Dan, but everything is wet. Soaking wet.'

'Not everything.' Dan snapped spindly twigs off the trunk of their conifer. 'See? Bone dry.'

Pushing apart the low branches, he stood up and began re-packing his pack. 'Let's explore!'

Inside the tree line, parallel to the shore, the densely branched conifers sheltered them from the weather. The ground was damp though and they were being dripped on relentlessly.

'An umbrella would be nice,' said Minnie.

Dan pulled up a large fern and handed it to her.

Laughing, she held it aloft. 'Perfect.'

The conifers opened up and they entered a glade of low-growing aspens, willows and shaggy wet bushes. Next they came upon a ridge with a game trail running up through the scrub. Walking the trail they could see grey sections of rock had dropped away, leaving a flat cliff face with fissures sprouting ferns, and a network of exposed brown roots that belonged to the trees on top.

'Somewhere way, way up there on the mountain, is the tree I saw get hit by lightning that day.'

'Which day?'

'The day we found the Bigfoot footprints.'

'Was it?'

'Yes, the day we saw that plane … the one that drops water on fires.'

'Ah yes, the day we saw the Super Scooper, the Bombardier 415. Great plane.'

Looking up at the rockface, Dan said, 'There must be a way up there. Let's take a closer look. Might find some good shelter.'

The game trail up the side of the ridge was well trodden, with deer prints showing clearly in the soft ground. The trail climbed up and over the rock outcrop where, lying across it, they found a massive decomposing redwood. Its topside was shoulder high to Dan. Clearly animals had climbed or jumped up and over the trunk, as there were scrabble marks and piles of loose red-brown bark on the grass. Beyond the fallen tree were endless tall pines and shaggy conifers.

Dan pushed through some bushes. 'Hey Minnie, look at this!'

He'd found the root-stump of the fallen redwood and it was enormous. Broken, snapped roots stuck out above them. It was like looking into the underside of a giant brown sea anemone. The centre of the stump, the very heart of the trunk, had rotted away and been devoured by bugs, beetles, worms and fungi. They stood together inside it, looking out at the rain.

'This came down a long time ago,' said Dan. 'This is ancient.' Small ferns were growing inside the vast, empty stump. Dan's outstretched hands just about touched both sides.

'Let's camp in here,' Minnie suggested. They immediately set to pulling up the ferns and clearing the ground.

From this elevated position inside the giant stump, on the steep sloping ridge above the shoreline, they had a commanding view of the beach and the bay.

'Just a short walk to the beach to collect firewood,' said Dan, 'and it's sheltered from the wind. Perfect.'

Minnie looked at the shore, what she could see of it, and up to the sky. The wind was blowing in even darker clouds.

'Yeah. Not looking good up there. Right! A fire!' said Dan, and he began to shove a row of sticks into the earth in front of the stump. He scooped out the ground to a few inches deep.

'Fireplace,' he announced. 'Let's gather kindling, Minnie.'

From inside the low branches of the nearest conifer they gathered handfuls of dry twigs, piling them by the scooped-out fireplace. They found larger fairly dry branches, and sticks and twigs under bushes, which they carried and dragged back to their camp.

Selecting a stick about as thick as Minnie's wrist, Dan whittled with his knife, making shavings from it which fell on the jacket he'd spread on the ground.

'Wanna try?' He offered her his camp knife, and she copied what Dan had done, cutting short curls of dry wood.

Wind and rain still battered the trees, rattling their branches together. The rustling of the wind-blown limbs would dwindle to a whisper, then suddenly intensify, almost drowning out their words. It hadn't escaped Minnie's notice that while Dan was busying himself with fire-prep he kept glancing up and around, into the forest. She sensed his unease.

'That enough?'

Dan scooped up the pile of shavings.

'Sure is.'

He placed them carefully on the thin, dry

twigs. Handing her the fire-starter rod and sheltering the shavings from the rain with his hands, he said, 'Go ahead.'

'How?'

'Just scrape the back of the knife down the ferro rod.'

She tried it and white sparks flew.

'Yes!'

Kneeling down, she put the rod in amongst the shavings and scraped the back edge of the knife down it. Dan knelt low to the pile, and as she scraped, sparks flew on to the shavings. Dan blew gently, and a small flame flickered.

'I did it!' Minnie laughed. 'I did it!'

Dan piled more tiny twigs on the flame. 'Minnie grab some of the pencil-sized twigs.'

They'd made separate piles – from pencil thick, finger thick, banana thick, to thick as her arm. They fed the fire with increasingly large twigs and when it was fully ablaze Dan lifted on a log that he'd stripped clean of its wet bark. They crouched down on their haunches inside the stump, admiring their blazing fire.

Dan handed Minnie a sandwich then twisted the top off the thermos flask.

Minnie munched.

'Bigfoot Mountain has disappeared.'

Dan looked across the choppy waters of the bay.

'Oh yeah, it's gone.'

The cloud had smothered the mountain completely.

'Hey, did you bring binoculars, Dan?'

He stopped chewing his sandwich, with a guilty expression.

'I'm not much of a boy scout after all.'

An hour later most of their gear was dry. They'd strung cord that, of course, Dan had in his pack, and hung their wet clothes in front of the fire.

Dan slipped his knife in its sheath. 'I sure hope your Bigfoot pal appreciates the effort we're making.'

Minnie hoisted her red backpack.

'He does.'

Dan rubbed his damp hair.

'I wish my hat hadn't blown into the sea.'

They set off down the trail to the beach. The

heavy rain was easing slightly but the wind was still strong, churning the waters of the bay roughly.

Dan scanned the terrain, looking for suitable firewood, as Minnie scanned the terrain looking for something else – tracks. In her hand she held her special measuring stick.

'If they snap when you break it, it means it's dry inside.' Dan grabbed up some twigs, snapped them, and shoved them into his backpack.

On the shoreline by the high-tide mark of seaweed and driftwood, Dan rolled the canoe right side up and unhooked the bailer.

'Good thing this is tin and not plastic.'

Minnie held the bailer by its thin handle. 'Why?'

'This is what we're going to cook with.' The tin was about the size of a small saucepan.

'Cook what?'

Dan cast his arms wide theatrically and said, 'Your dinner awaits you.'

Minnie did the same, sweeping her arms out and, remembering something Connie had said she declared, 'When the tide is out, the table is laid.'

They walked towards the far end of the beach,

the forest to their right, the sea to their left. What looked like soft, crumbling grey rock extending out from the forest onto the beach was hard to the touch, pitted and jagged, with weird round scoops worn by the weather. The pits made it easy to climb and they clambered up and over it easily. On the other side were dozens of tidal pools, some small and shallow, others larger and deeper, and in many were black, spiny sea urchins, and pink and orange sea anemones. In most of the pools, small fish flitted round and round, and from side to side.

'Well, there's plenty of cockles and limpets.' Dan squatted, examining a pool closely.

'And crabs.' Minnie reached in and pulled a crab out of the water. She dropped it back in.

'Hey, look.' Dan was pointing at the lump of rock they had clambered over. The underside, below the overhang, was covered in mussels – shiny, black, thousands of them. 'Wow!'

Dan wrenched some loose, dropping them in his backpack.

'What about if I leave it up there.' Minnie was pointing to the jagged rock they'd just climbed over. 'It's high enough that the tide won't take it.'

'The quartz? Sure.' Dan looked up at the rocky

outcrop. 'Looks good to me. They'll be able to see it and it won't get washed away.'

Dan collected more mussels, some clams and limpets, as Minnie climbed back up the pitted grey outcrop. Shrugging it loose, she unzipped the backpack and pulled out the lump of quartz. Turning to face the forest, she held it aloft in two hands. The steep hills were so densely forested there was not a patch of ground to be seen.

At the top of her voice she yelled, 'This is for you! This is for you! He needs you! He needs your help!'

She placed it carefully, making sure the bloodstain was on the underside so the rain couldn't easily wash it away.

Minnie felt good because it felt like the right thing to do. She couldn't be sure they were watching her and Dan, or that they were even on this side of the island, but she was sure this is what her Bigfoot friend wanted her to do.

They headed back along the beach.

'Do you think they'll come while we're here, Dan, or wait till we leave?'

'Hmm, good question. Wait till we leave? Or maybe come back with us in the canoe?'

'They couldn't do that. There's a hole in the canoe!'

'Oh. Yeah. I might be able to patch that.'

'Really?'

'Er, sure, with like, birch bark, and some pine pitch.'

'Pine pitch?'

'Yeah. To make a kind of glue.'

'How much pine pitch?'

'A handful or so. Melt it in a pot, mix it with some ash. Easy. We only have one pot though and we need that for food.'

'Maybe we'll just wait for Sam.'

'Yeah, we'll wait for Sam.'

Dan grabbed up a sand-smeared and dented plastic bottle. 'We'll need some seawater for cooking.' He jogged down the beach to the sea.

Minnie stood alone and slowly turned to look up at the forest – the line of tall, dense firs and redwoods stood sentinel before her, as if guarding the secrets of the forest. She had no sense of being watched at that moment, but still couldn't help quickly scanning the gaps between the trees; there was a part of her that really did not want to see the face of a Bigfoot looking back at her.

Back at the camp, Dan dumped the driftwood he'd lugged back from the beach into a pile, and set to cutting some green boughs off the conifers, while Minnie got the fire going again.

'Right, Minnie, this green stuff has got moisture in the needles, so it will create smoke. We want smoke to signal to Billy and Connie.'

'Right. Cool. Will they see it OK?'

'I think so. The clouds have passed. It's just the wind making the water way too rough to cross. Alex will be so mad if Sam doesn't make it back today!'

'If Sam does make it back, will he come and look for us, Dan? Connie will tell him we didn't return, right? She'll be worried.'

'Alex will probably tell him to forget about us and head back to the nearest airport!'

'So, Alex would leave us here?'

'Not up to Alex. It's Sam's boat. He would come over here for sure if he could. So don't worry. If we send a smoke signal they'll know we survived the crossing, and that we're here and we're well enough to build a fire. Yes? All good?'

'All good,' Minnie poked the fire. 'But it would be nice if Billy and Connie were here too.'

'Yes, it would.' Dan piled green boughs on the fire and a cloud of grey smoke quickly formed and rose curling up through the pines.

Dan cut more. 'If they're looking through binoculars they should see the smoke.'

Minnie glanced up at a billowing bank of cloud. 'Let's keep it going until it gets dark.'

'We will,' Dan assured her.

From where they were they couldn't see the rocks they'd left the quartz on, but Minnie kept scanning the section of the beach they could see from their camp on the ridge. She knew they wouldn't come while she was watching but she was worried more about her Bigfoot than she was about Alex's state of mind, or Sam's whereabouts, or even Connie and Billy's anxiety. She felt that his family, who were somewhere here on this island, would somehow know she was here to help.

Dan dropped a load of mussels in the tin bailer and topped it up with seawater from the discarded plastic bottle. He rested the bailer on the fire. Dan opened one of the squares of space blanket, like kitchen foil but stronger, and thinner, it crinkled and crackled as he spread it.

'When we turn in you can wrap yourself in the blanket and I'll cover you with the space blanket, Min. Tuck you in tight.'

'Snug as a bug in a rug?'

'You got it.'

'Dan?'

'Yes, Minnie.'

'You know that feeling we got in the forest?'

'Er, when?'

'Like, whenever we went in the forest, back home?'

'Well, the first time they threw a pinecone at me, and the next…'

'Up at the Giant X.'

'Up at the Giant X they clacked rocks and pushed a tree over, so yes, I remember the feeling. Scary.'

'I don't have a feeling now, a feeling like we're being watched.'

'You don't?'

'No. Do you?'

'No. No, I don't.'

'Good.'

'Yes, good! Maybe we'll get a sweet night's sleep under the star-sprinkled sky!' Kneeling by the fire, and with a grin, Dan swept his arm up to the sky.

Minnie smiled, and peered up at the sky. 'I think it might rain, Dan.'

'Oh. Yeah.' Dan looked up then, as he did every minute or so, into the trees. He poked the fire with a stick, and faintly, at the very edge of his hearing, he heard what sounded like the hoot of an owl.

KAAYII

Chapter Seven

So strong was Kaayii's connection with the animals of the forest that, as he sat high in the tree thinking of his crow friend's passing, he was joined by a dozen honeybees, two white butterflies and a reddish-brown hummingbird. They circled his head in tight formation three times and then buzzed off, fluttered by, and hummed away home. Kaayii thanked them.

There she was, the girl he now knew as Minnie, standing on the jetty looking down at the two small boats. No one else with her, not even the dog. Kaayii watched keenly as she climbed down on to the muddy shore, leaned over one of the boats, reached down and lifted up the quartz. To Kaayii's astonishment she turned to face the mountain, lifted the quartz in both hands and did a funny little dance.

Smiling, he watched her hurry across the grey sand, scramble up the rocks on to the grass and run back to her cabin.

So there he sat, patiently, in the highest crook of the pine tree, waiting to see what the girl would do next. He peeled strips of bark with his strong black fingers to chew on, carefully stripping off the edible soft layer. The pine swayed. The lightening sky and swiftly scudding clouds from the southwest brought the threat of rain.

Kaayii caught a splash of white spray beyond the small, wooded islands and wondered if it was the seal, just as Minnie and her father emerged from the cabin. They walked down to the beach. She pointed at the sand and they crouched down to study the wolf prints. They searched the beach and the mud for more prints, then Minnie ran up the grassy slope with the quartz, and her father went back to the cabin. Kaayii watched as Minnie visited the cabin near the forest and stood on the deck talking for a while with the small boy he now knew was called Billy, and his mother.

Soon her father joined them there. Minnie ran off down the slope and her father hurried after her, and Kaayii could sense they were not in agreement.

They both walked down to their cabin and went inside. Kaayii wondered if she understood what the quartz in the boat had meant; if she understood his message.

When Minnie and her father eventually came out of the cabin they were carrying bags. The man had a big black bag and the girl had a smaller red bag.

The boy, Billy, and his mother walked down and joined them. The adult humans disappeared behind the small cabin and Kaayii wondered what they were doing there but soon they re-appeared carrying a slim green boat with curved pointed ends.

Close to the jetty they lowered it onto the water. Kaayii couldn't see the quartz. He hoped it was in her bag.

He watched all these comings and goings with fascination – he never got bored with watching humans. He wondered why they all lived in separate wooden boxes, but then thought that maybe the woman and Minnie's father could be brother and sister. Or that Minnie's mother had passed, unless she was on a visit to another clan, but she had been gone for a long time now.

He was still pondering human ways of life when the slim, older boy walked down the grass to the jetty with his mother. Lastly, the man came into view strolling down the path to the jetty to join the others. The man did not show them the doll or point over to the boat where he'd found it, and Kaayii wondered what he had done with the twisted-willow figure, the gift he had made for Minnie.

Kaayii watched as the group of seven humans talked for a while, then Minnie and her father got in the canoe and paddled away. He was thrilled when they kept paddling past the small tree-tufted islands, heading directly out across the bay towards the big island.

His thoughts returned to the Grey – he wondered where the troubled old Sasquatch was. The forest was deathly silent. Kaayii listened carefully. He could hear no damage being done in the woods and could not feel his angry presence anywhere nearby. Then far away, deep in the forest, he sensed a crack, and a few seconds later, relayed from the network of roots, up the trunk of the tree he was sitting in, he felt the earth shudder, as somewhere not that far away a very large tree hit the ground.

Usually the wolves would sleep in the nest of moss and ferns at the Watcher's Place, but the odour left by the Grey was so strong and so unpleasant, even to a wolf, that they'd trotted away to a mulberry bush and were lying under it when Kaayii dropped down from his pine tree.

The trail left by the Grey was easy to follow. Often Sasquatches will not use game trails when travelling through forests. They are so big and tall they can step over obstacles, and they simply push aside or break branches in their way. Being able to sense the movement of creatures in the forest, and not just rely on sight and sound, they can lie in wait for animals using the trails.

The Grey, however, was behaving so roguishly and out of tune with the rhythm and pulse of the forest that he'd marched up hills and down trails in long heavy strides, leaving deep footprints in the ground, breaking branches twice the height of a human from the ground, lifting and hoiking heavy logs and tree trunks out of the way, leaving an angry path of destruction in his wake.

Kaayii and the wolves increased their pace.

Creatures of the forest appeared, bolting past them. Animals that normally would keep away from the Sasquatch broke cover, running past Kaayii and the wolves in panic. Pine martens and weasels scurried along branches. A raccoon rushed past them. Squirrels called 'cheek-cheek' in the high treetops. A bobcat bounded by. The wolves stopped, turning instinctively, wanting to chase the short-tailed cat with black-tipped ears, but Kaayii called them on with a soft whistle.

A blue jay streaked out of the trees. A woodpecker, a raven, two doves, an owl and a squadron of black-capped chickadees flew by, looking for an easy escape up through the tangle of tree branches, out to the clear safe sky.

CRASH! Breaking branches beyond the next rise resounded through the forest followed by a conclusively loud *THUD!*

Kaayii stopped by a broad cedar, its high-buttressed trunk spread wide and, peering down the gully beyond, he caught a glimpse of a massive grey figure walking through a stand of silver birch trees. At the bottom of the gully of scrub-willow, where a spring had filled a shallow, muddy hollow, was the tree the Grey had pushed down. It was a mature cottonwood. The moss-covered straight brown trunk was now detached from its top half, which had shattered on impact flinging branches and split bark all around. Kaayii lost sight of the Grey when he seemed to simply fade away, into the shadows of the bushes beyond the birch trees.

Kaayii and the wolves hurried through the silver birches and up the other side of the wide gully to the top of the bluff, and there he was, crouched beside a blackberry bush. Feeding on the berries, the Grey kept straightening up to peek over the top of the bush. He was stalking something.

Running had made Kaayii's head hurt. Though it had stopped bleeding, thanks to the cattail gel, it was still raw where the Grey had hit him with the quartz. Kaayii reached into the branches of the nearest silver birch tree. He broke off thin twigs and leaves. Stuffing a handful in his huge mouth, he munched down with his big square teeth. He pushed more leaves in and chewed, keeping an eye on the Grey. When he had pulped the birch mass enough, his mouth spilling saliva down his chin, he swallowed it, knowing in a short while the ache in his head would ease.

The Grey unfolded himself from where he'd

been crouching and stood looking straight ahead. Now Kaayii could see what he was stalking. It was a young bull moose. Kaayii had never seen moose this close to the shoreline, but the fires that had ravaged the range beyond the mountains had driven many of the larger creatures to these lush slopes. Kaayii recognised the broad, flat antlers, each with seven rounded points. This was the offspring of the moose that the wolf pack from the north had killed, the moose who was Kaayii's father's friend.

Smooth brown velvet covered the antlers, which gleamed in the afternoon sun. His long slim head, the huge ears constantly twitching and swivelling, was longer than a horse's. It ended with a protruding upper lip that was useful for pulling young shoots and leaves off the branches of birch, maple, aspen and poplar.

Kaayii knew what the Grey would do next – he would produce a low vibration deep in his chest, directing it at the moose who would stand dazed and confused, and might then topple over, or might just stand there while the Grey rushed at him, broke his neck with his massive arms, and ripped him apart to feed on.

The low hum began. Kaayii told the wolves, their ears pricked forward, to stay where they were. He ran down the gully and up the other side to where fir trees grew, with cylindrical dark purple cones sitting on their branches in clusters. Kaayii plucked three cones off a branch and ran stealthily towards the Grey. The Grey kept his full attention and focus on the young moose, as Kaayii crept up behind it until he was in range.

Trees were dotted about between Kaayii and the moose, and he had to shift his position so he had a clear shot. He hurled the first cone. It fell short, bouncing past the moose, standing still as a statue. He threw again with all his throwing might. It hit the moose on his antler, snapping it out of his zombie-like reverie. The third hit his flank, and the moose leapt into the air, suddenly seeing the Grey, his survival instincts kicking in. He bolted in a mad panic, eyes bulging, mouth gaping, straight down the slope through the trees towards the sea.

Now the old Sasquatch was looking straight at Kaayii, black eyes drilling into the young Sasquatch's soul.

There was a loud splash as the young moose

launched himself into the water, and began frantically swimming away. Under the surface his four legs cantered, driving his sleek body smoothly through the water, but his bulging eyes and his flaring nostrils signalled his fear.

Kaayii ran. The wolves followed.

Behind them, crashing through the forest, they could hear the Grey in hot pursuit of Kaayii. A herd of deer higher up the slope pelted through a pine grove at full gallop, throwing up a flurry of leaves and twigs. Quickly catching up to the deer, fearful and wild-eyed, running for their lives, Kaayii joined them, wanting their prints to disguise his own tracks. Heading up the mountain, he hoped the Grey would give up the chase, or be distracted by the deer. Kaayii stopped behind a large boulder and listened, crouching low, steadying his breathing. The deer's noisy retreat faded into the forest, and silence reigned.

Chapter Eight

A cold wind hustled through the underbrush, as Kaayii sat amongst the high red-and-orange twisted branches of an arbutus tree. The peaks of the island across the bay were shrouded in cloud and, though the sun shone onto this side of the bay, the breeze carried the threat of rain.

The forest stretched steeply behind him, and Kaayii felt sure he would sense the Grey's presence if he ventured down the lower slopes. He hoped the humans were not making enticing food smells as they sometimes did, which could draw in any Sasquatch within smelling distance, which for a Sasquatch was a long way – not as far as some bears but much further than humans could smell.

Kaayii had a perfect view of the closest cabin, its deck draped with sweet-smelling white flowers. He could hear the hum of the bees busy amongst the twining greenery. It was late afternoon. The dark-haired woman stood on the deck. Billy and the dog were elsewhere. Kaayii wondered if they were collecting mussels and cockles on the shore, as he had so often watched them do.

The woman went inside the cabin and quickly returned to her position on the deck. She raised something black to her eyes and held it to her face. She lowered it, looking far out across the bay then raised it again to her eyes. Kaayii wondered what it was she was doing. Humans carry so much with them, wherever they go, so he wasn't surprised to see yet more bizarre behaviour.

He remembered when his father and uncle had joined Kaayii in the three tall pines near the Watcher's Place to spend days watching the girl's father remove the wooden box structure they slept in, until only the thick standing posts remained. The structure was full of bewildering things none of the Sasquatches could identify – colourful, strangely shaped, big and small.

The woman picked up a smaller black object from the table, looked at it in her hand, poked it with her finger a few times and held it to her ear. It was the same size as the black thing the man had pointed at the wolf tracks on the beach earlier.

Kaayii was so close that if he had coughed the woman would have turned to look for the source of the noise. Kaayii had had a drink at the stream in the grove, had found some berries and some mushrooms and had taken a long drink again where the stream disappeared in the pipe under the road, but he knew if he relieved himself from up in the tree she would hear the splashing on the dry leaves, so he decided to wait until she went inside before climbing down as quietly as he could. But she didn't go inside. She hurried down the steps with the black object hanging from her neck by straps and the smaller black object in her hand.

Kaayii climbed down and slipped away into the tall underbrush behind the cabin. A little while later, he leant out from behind a tree and looked up and down the hiking trail. No humans in sight – with one bound he was in the trees on the other side.

The long white blades of the wind-turbine spun in a blur. Its tripod of sturdy steel legs was bolted to the rock on which it stood. Kaayii sat behind one of the four shiny black panels also bolted to the rock. This new position afforded an even better view of the cabins and the humans staying in them.

Kaayii surveyed the scene. The humans were on the jetty. The small boy and the taller boy were sitting on the end with fishing lines dangling in the sea. Their hair and their shirts ruffled by the breeze, they seemed content. The three adults seemed less happy. The black-haired woman kept pointing at the big island, at the approaching dark clouds, and brandishing the small black object in her hand. She seemed worried.

The man, the man who'd taken Minnie's gift from the dinghy, was very angry about something, and he yelled at the two women. The yellow-haired one marched up to their cabin and the black-haired one walked to the end of the jetty gazing out across the choppy waves. The man stood alone. He stamped his foot on the ground in exactly the way Kaayii's little sister would do when she was told to stop eating all the berries and to wait for the others.

Across the bay sheeting grey rain now doused the island, and racing wind churned the water. Minnie and her father would have got to the other side by now, he thought. Had they decided to stay there? He hoped not – the mountain would be a much less special place if the girl went away.

Something caught his eye. Was that the faintest smudge of pale grey smoke, low in the woods near the shoreline of the big island?

Kaayii curled his knees to his chest and waited until nightfall in a damp heap, as rain crashed noisily on the slick, black panels. The moon had long-since faded from view behind the dense cloud when the bedraggled Sasquatch rolled out from under the solar panels. The cabins were dark and had been for a while.

He heard rustling nearby in the brush, and a sodden water rat darted away, startled to find a huge hairy being on the rocky outcrop.

Kaayii studied the way the water of the bay was behaving in the storm. The surface heaved, the waves danced in the squalling wind. The tide was at its height. Kaayii knew from watching with his father that after it reached its highest point, the sea would slacken a while, waiting, before it receded again, but in this weather, the tide could be much higher than usual, and going out the tide would have more energy. He was worried.

He decided to test the strength of the sea. Climbing down the slippery rocks to the water, he dived headfirst into the heaving swell. The tide was pulling, but he was strong enough to swim against it, heading for the end of the jetty. He dived deep and felt the swaying kelp brush his legs.

He let the waves push him closer to the shore. Heaving himself out he stood dripping by the jetty, looking out into the darkness.

Now that he was lower down and closer to the water, Kaayii hoped he would sense the approach of his father, swimming towards him any moment now.

Surely the Sasquatches would have been watching Minnie and her father, on the big island, and would have been drawn to the power of the crystal. Surely they would know it meant Kaayii needed help.

He sat on the shore, chewing some kelp, and his father's voice spoke in his mind: *Kaayii.*

The young Sasquatch stood and glimpsed four dark heads between the waves just beyond the smaller island. His heart soared.

Soon, near the tall bushes by the stream, Kaayii was being held in the shared embrace of four Sasquatches – his father Taashi, his uncle Ahniiq, and a pair from his clan, Ahnoosh and Yaaqwun. They each, in turn, touched their forehead to Kaayii's. Yaaqwun gently put a fingertip to the wound on his head and nudged his shoulder with her head to show sympathy. Not a word had been spoken.

Kaayii began to lead the four across the road and up the path by the stream to the grove, but his father took his arm to stop him, and pointed up the track that passed the cabins. So the five Sasquatches walked in silence, making barely a sound as they padded slowly up the narrow rain-soaked track, past Minnie's favourite pine tree, past the fenced garden and its aromas of sweet, rich earth and burgeoning fruit, past the standing posts they had crept through to get to the jetty weeks ago, and up the track towards the forest.

At Connie and Billy's cabin Taashi stopped and placed his hand on the cabin wall, smiling at his son. This time he didn't whack the side with his massive hand as he had before.

When they reached the trail that left the track,

and led up to the Watcher's Place, they advanced in single file, each leaving a gap of about ten steps.

They gathered at the Watcher's Place, where there was no sign of the Grey. The Sasquatches circled Kaayii as he chose his words and spoke the ancient language melodiously, stating, 'The old Grey took the life of my fine crow friend by this tree. I feared his rage. I stayed to protect the humans.'

They continued up the trail. Listening to the sounds of the forest and the energy shifting around them, they moved in silence through the Aspen Grove.

They paused at the Giant X, the tripod and the teepee, the tree trunks now a scattered mess littering the forest floor. They sat together by the quartz outcrop, near the first ravine, listening and waiting, but they could not feel the angry presence of the Grey anywhere near them.

Well-chosen words were needed to explain why he had brought the four back to the mountain. 'He hit me with the quartz near the giant tree.' Kaayii pointed at the biggest redwood in the forest. 'Down near the shore he hunted the young moose.'

Kaayii led the way straight up the mountain, over the second ravine where he had found the injured Minnie. They passed the tree where his mother had nursed the girl, putting pine resin on her cuts and where they'd watched over her as she slept.

Persistent rain fell as five large dark heads appeared to float above the shoulder-high grass on the open meadow. Passing Kaayii's favourite tall tree, they entered the dense thicket at High Ridge.

At the far end of the ridge, by the quartz outcrop with a view of the bay through the spruce, poplars and pines, they stood around the moss-covered grave, with its neat circle of stones. 'The Grey pulled your mother's tree up and tore away the moss.'

They held hands as they stood around her resting place, and remembered his grandmother, Shweya.

They stood in a line facing the cave. The rain had eased, and the trees dripped, as did the Sasquatches. Clouds had parted, blown north by the sea breeze. Silver moonlight patterned the underbrush through the tall spruce pines that shielded the cave entrance from view. Tangled creepers looped from the escarpment above into the tops of the swaying pines.

Without entering the cave, they knew the Grey was inside. Taashi howled a short but very loud howl. Their gaze was fixed on the gap behind the boulder that Taashi and Ahniiq had heaved clear of the entrance when Kaayii had first discovered this cave.

Moments later the massive figure of the Grey emerged. He paused as he studied the group of five then strode slowly down the winding path through the boulder field towards them.

Only when he stepped clear of the last shoulder-high rock could they see that he was carrying a wolf in each hand, held tight by the scruff of the neck, as they kicked out in protest and fear.

Yaaqwun took a step forward, and she asked by thought alone: *why are you here?* The Grey returned a perfect gaze of blankness.

Taashi snarled as he communicated: *you must leave this place and be part of another forest.*

The Grey released his grip on the two wolves.

They promptly bolted through the underbrush, their tails between their legs. He stepped forward into a shaft of moonlight, and it was then that the Sasquatches could see how old he was. Though taller and broader than any of them, and clearly of immense physical power, his face was heavily lined under the short grey hair, and folds of skin hung about his eyes, chin and neck. To Kaayii he looked weary, his shoulders slumped, and he swayed slightly back and forth. The Grey may have felt Kaayii's assessment, and he stiffened his posture, adding several inches to his height by doing so. He looked from one to the other, wary, alert to attack.

Yaaqwun took a step towards the Grey and smiled, silently stating: *I sense anger and sorrow.*

All five of the Sasquatches before him, asked the same question by thought alone: *why?*

After again receiving no reply, Kaayii's uncle Ahniiq took a step forward.

Moonlight cast the Grey as a magnificent silver effigy, yet Kaayii sensed pride in the ancient forest being and also, somewhere deep within him, a yawning chasm of loss that touched the young Sasquatch's heart.

The Grey held Ahniiq's searching gaze then dropped his head back, looked up to the eternal black of night, opened his mouth and roared a powerful howl of grief and torment. The echo rolled around the escarpment repeating off the high granite outcrop. The Grey, still gazing skyward murmured simple words, which meant, 'The fire took them.'

Ahniiq raised his hand and asked: *how many died in the fire?*

The Grey levelled his gaze at the five. Perhaps sensing in them a compassion he felt he didn't deserve, the Grey to Kaayii seemed on the point of succumbing to emotions beyond his control, and indeed the Grey's lips trembled and he grimaced, squelching his eyes in folds of black skin. He lifted his vast hands, palms forward, stretching the ten digits wide.

The forest beings slowly advanced, encircling the Grey. They shuffled closer together, arms outstretched, closing the circle, and hummed a song of love, as they held the Grey in their forgiving embrace.

Kaayii led the five Sasquatches rapidly down the mountain through the Fern Grove, not wanting to risk exciting the Grey by passing close to the humans' cabins.

When they emerged from the thick underbrush to cross the road in single file, with the Grey in the middle of the chain, a thick fog had begun to spread, silently blanketing the bay. As Kaayii turned to look back at his mountain, the fog had turned the face of the forest to a ghostly pallor, low wisps of pale grey nestling amongst the trees.

Kaayii was behind the Grey, who stopped and turned. For the first time he saw the humans' cabins. He grunted with surprise. Looking at Kaayii he pointed at the structures. Kaayii just smiled and encouraged him on by gently pushing his shoulder.

On the shoreline, shingle and mud had been exposed by the receding tide. Aware of leaving prints, but having weighed the risk, they followed Taashi in single file between boulders and tide pools to the shallows, keeping the old Grey in the middle of the group. Kaayii dropped back.

Stepping up onto the grassy bank, he stood still, squarely in front of the cabin on the little rise and thought of the man who had Minnie's gift. He focused his energy on the human inside...

The man and the yellow-haired woman were sleeping in a big flat square bed. The man was snoring. He stopped with a snort and turned, rolling on to his back and, briefly opening his eyes, he looked to the door. The Sasquatch's head touched the ceiling and his shoulders filled the doorframe. The man closed his eyes sleepily. His eyes snapped open, abject terror etched on his face. The Sasquatch was gone.

Kaayii stood on the grass, looking up at the cabin, thinking of the man and Minnie's gift. He slowly turned to face the bay and hurried back down to the water.

The first hint of dawn was creeping up the silhouetted mountain range in the east, as the group of six swam together past the little pine-topped island.

'Unghhhh!' A very loud quavering grunt rent the damp night air. Followed by 'Ouaahhh!'–a loud, prolonged cough.

Kaayii peered into the dark at the larger of the small islands and could make out, lurking in the shadows of the wind-bent pines, the pathetic lone figure of the young bull moose. He was gazing gloomily at the Sasquatches swimming past the island.

Spotting the Grey amongst the group of six, the bull moose bellowed, 'Unghhh!' Horrified to see the Grey again, he lolloped away from the edge to the far side of the island.

Kaayii called out a greeting to it, 'Oosh!'

The moose, recognising Kaayii, carefully stepped closer to the edge of the island.

'Oosh!' Kaayii called again. Encouraged, and unhappy with island life, the young moose took the first of many daring decisions he'd make in his life, and leapt in to the sea, sending a moonlit splash arcing across the water – *SHPLOOMPFF!*

Kicking madly, eyes bulging, he joined Kaayii and the other Sasquatches, as they swam together, powering through the water with massive feet and strong legs.

Halfway across the tidal inlet, the six swimming Sasquatches and the young bull moose were joined by Kaayii's new friend the black seal, who effortlessly twisted and dived around and under the group. The rain was easing and the moon, though not yet full, lit the waves in a rippling silver sheen. The outgoing tide had forced the group in a southerly arc, closer to the furthest point of the island. As their feet touched sand and rocks, they waded out of the waves.

The tide, though only halfway out, had exposed a spur of beach. Taashi and Kaayii's uncle strode up the sand heading straight for the headland of high grey rocks. They were followed by Yaaqwun and Ahnoosh, who helped the Grey find his feet and held hands with him as they left the water.

The seal nudged Kaayii with his snout as he stood waist deep in the waves. He held something in his whiskered mouth. With a flick of his head, he flung it at Kaayii, who swept it up with his massive hand. It was a man's blue cap. Kaayii turned to thank the seal, but he had already slipped away.

The bedraggled young moose stood dripping on the gravelly spit of land, his head hung low in exhaustion. Kaayii pointed at the treeline, and told him: *food*. The moose plodded slowly away from the sea.

The rain had stopped, the clouds had parted and the Sasquatches were waiting for Kaayii in the moon shadow cast by the high rocky headland. Cut between the island and the limestone headland was a short canyon where sea stacks, like tall stone towers, stood amongst the puddles and pools of the shallows.

Taashi pointed ahead and Kaayii stepped forward, holding the cap loosely in one hand, followed by the others. Enjoying the new sensation of the coarse pink sand between his toes he strode through the canyon, leading the group. Taashi pointed the way again, indicating a jagged, pockmarked rock. Kaayii, in two moves, climbed up and stood on the rock promontory looking down on the precious quartz embraced by its tangle of roots. Smiling, he silently thanked Minnie for bringing it safely across the water.

Near the rock stacks in the canyon at the base of the cliff, among a jumble of sea-loosened boulders, was a gap in the rock face. Taashi led the way. Sasquatches are nocturnal, so can see at night, but they struggle to see in complete darkness. As they climbed into a passage the light grew dimmer until they were feeling their way. The Sasquatches ahead of Kaayii had memorised the route, and their steps didn't falter. Ahniiq held Kaayii's hand and Yaaqwun guided him from behind, helping him to place his feet safely. They chatted as they climbed. His father and uncle explained about the tides around the island, and the plentiful seafood.

His uncle Ahniiq communicated one strong thought to Kaayii: *oysters*.

Kaayii laughed. His uncle had always loved oysters.

Kaayii could see a hint of moonlight in the cave ahead. Following a path between boulders, they climbed higher, towards the light. Squeezing through a gap in the passage, they were able to stand up straight in a vast echoing cavern.

Dawn was breaking through a jagged opening in the rock ceiling, and Kaayii could see now where they were going. Below the crack of light, and brightening by the minute, was a large flat area with shadowy arched openings. Hundreds of stalactites, looking like creamy icicles, covered the ceiling of the vast space where water had seeped through the limestone and had dripped for millions of years. Leaving a tiny deposit of calcium with each drip, stalagmites had grown up from the floor, directly below each stalactite, and Kaayii gazed at the beautiful, strange shapes and the pointed shadows they cast.

Taashi, Ahniiq, Yaaqwun and Ahnoosh stood to one side and gently pushed Kaayii forward. Ahnoosh made a clucking, warbling sound by flapping his lips as he sang high-pitched notes, a bit like a chicken trying to sing opera. It was a Sasquatch song of greeting. The Grey lurked behind the others in the dark.

Sasquatches appeared from the side caverns. Enksi and Wesh, the oldest couple, emerged from the nearest large gap in the rock. They embraced Kaayii. His little sister Yaluqwa came running out of another passage and jumped at her brother, squealing with delight. Ahnoosh and Yaaqwun's daughter, Shumsha, walked from the shadows and embraced her parents and Kaayii.

Yumiqsu, Kaayii's mother, hurried out of her cave amid much laughter and tears, as she approached her son. She looked up into his black eyes, and they touched foreheads. She rested her hands on his broad shoulders and gave a low gentle hum.

Sensing a strange energy in the space, Kaayii's mother drew back from Kaayii and looked around. Her eyes found and rested on the Grey, still standing apart from the group in the shadowy recesses of the cavern. As she studied his face, what she could see of it, a silence fell on the group, and they stepped back to allow the Grey into the gathering.

The immense grey Sasquatch returned her gaze, and the expression on her face altered from one of curiosity, to a deepening recognition.

MINNIE

Chapter Nine

It had rained most of the night. Rainwater had dripped through the conifer branches they'd placed across the top of the redwood stump and onto Minnie's silver space blanket. Each drop sounded like someone flicking the thin foil sheeting with a finger. Moisture lingered in the air and Minnie could smell the odours of wet earth, damp bark, seaweed, and the rising scent of pine.

Dan had re-lit the fire and was boiling some water in the tin bailer. Minnie groaned and twisted to relieve the pain from something jabbing her in the side. Arching her back, she yanked a small pine bough out from under her torso.

'Morning, Minnie. Rain's stopped. Sleep OK?'

'Well, I didn't sleep like a log, but OK, I guess.'

Vague memories of a dream lingered in her

mind. At home she often dreamt of her mother and lately of the creatures in the forest. She vaguely recalled dreaming about a black dog or a seal. Swimming and stormy waves featured strongly, which didn't surprise her after their eventful crossing. It wasn't a worrying dream, but she'd never dreamt of a seal before. Connie would know the significance of a seal, she thought, wriggling out of her blanket cocoon.

'Pine-needle tea, Min?'

'Maybe after, thanks.'

'After?'

'After I've checked on the quartz.'

'Oh.'

'Did you check on the quartz, Dan?'

'No.'

'Good. We can go together.'

'Yes, we can. Can I finish my tea?'

'Holy smokes!'

Minnie was looking out from their camp to where the sea should have been. She could see as far as the canoe, where they'd left it on the nearside of the pile of driftwood, and nothing beyond except a dense fog that had settled in the bay.

Dan looked out. 'I've never seen a fog like it.'

'Will Sam still come and get us?'

'Not safe to navigate in this fog, not in a boat that size. Too many rocks to hit.'

Minnie grinned as she put on her sneakers. 'Alex will be furious!'

'Yes, he will!'

Dan yanked on a windcheater jacket and grabbed Minnie's outstretched hand, heaving her to her feet.

She pulled on a sweater, tugged her measuring twig out of her backpack, and announced, 'Ready!'

Minnie ran along the firm pinky-grey sand following the high-tide mark of logs. Dan threw a stick into the fog. They didn't hear it land as the fog smothered the sound.

She looked for footprints but the sand had been levelled smooth and pristine by the receding tide. Slowing to a walk as she neared the jagged grey outcrop, she could see the top of the rock. Her heart sank. Dan joined her and put an arm across her shoulders.

'I don't think they'll come while we're still here,' he whispered.

'But we're trapped here,' Minnie murmured, on the point of tears. 'No one can rescue us because of the fog and we can't paddle because of our canoe, and my friend Rufus may be dying over on Bigfoot Mountain, and there's nothing we can do about it!'

'You've done everything you could do.'

Minnie climbed the rock. The quartz was exactly how she'd left it.

'Dan!'

'What is it?'

'Look.' He clambered up to join her.

Next to the quartz, held down with a pale pink stone about the size of a pinecone, was Dan's blue cap.

'Someone was here!' Minnie exclaimed.

'Wow!' said Dan, carefully lifting the stone to inspect his baseball cap.

'They didn't take the quartz, but they wanted us to know they'd found it!'

'Wow,' Dan repeated, still computing. 'Just … wow…'

'I know!' Minnie did her happy dance. Dan scratched his head, then pulled the cap on, grinning broadly.

'Your mom gave me this.'

Minnie flung her arms round him and they hugged and laughed.

'Wait,' she put her palm to his chest. 'We don't know if they saw the blood on the quartz and understood!'

'You're overthinking it, Minnie. They're probably over there now, doing … doing whatever it is they need to do.'

Minnie looked at Dan, considering. Dan knew to wait. Minnie liked to look at things from every angle, make a decision and stick to it. Dan had learned that about her in the short time since the whole Bigfoot thing had begun a few short weeks ago.

'OK,' she said. 'Let's explore.' She began to climb down the rock.

'Now?'

'What else is there to do?'

'Breakfast?'

'We'll collect some mussels on the way back.'

Jumping down on to the sand she strode off towards the far end of the beach, leaping over and around the many tide pools.

'Wait for me!'

Dan caught up with her. As they got closer to the headland, they realised that it was not really a headland at all, but was separate from the island. A canyon had been worn through the limestone rock, washed away piece by piece and pebble by pebble by thousands of years of relentless waves and weather.

Standing in the canyon were slim stacks of limestone as tall as the headland they'd been separated from, as tall as a house. Some had ferns growing in cracks, whose windborne spores had found a crevice to sprout from. There was a small, twisted oak growing on the top of one stack and a pine sapling on another. Minnie and Dan stood and gawped, astonished at the sight of towering plant-covered stacks standing amongst the tide pools on the smooth pink sand.

'I didn't know there were sea stacks here!' said Dan. 'Cool.'

Minnie was searching for footprints in the sand, or any sign of activity from the local residents.

'Sam said they saw three sets of footprints.'

Emerging from the gap between the headland and the cliff, the southernmost part of the island revealed itself as a wide stretch of immaculate beach, as wide as a football field – the far end of it invisible, hidden behind the fog.

'Will this fog burn off soon, Dan?'

'Should do, unless there are clouds blocking the sun.' Dan was looking at his phone, waving it around, trying for a signal.

Minnie waited for Dan to catch up with her, looking inland to where the layer of fog met the trees and dispersed among the tightly packed conifers. Dan was looking at the trees too. The tall, shaggy conifers grew close to the shoreline but there was a high ridge along the length of the beach, the face of which was concave, where the waves and tide had gnawed away at the land.

They were both still and silent for a while.

'Dan?'

'Yes, Minnie?'

'Are you feeling…?'

'Yes, I am.'

'Shall we head back?'

'Think we should.' And with that they turned and started walking back towards the gap in the limestone outcrop.

As they approached the sea stacks, they could

see the rock pools were almost all under water, as the tide washed in around the outcrop.

'Hurry, Minnie. The tide's coming in!'

'Why isn't it coming in here on the beach?' Minnie asked as they started running.

'It is! Behind the fog! There must be channels funnelling it through the canyon!'

They ran, and when they could run no more, they waded, with the stone promontory high on their right and the blunt face of the cliffs to their left. The tide seemed to be in a mighty rush to fill the gap with churning, rushing water.

'We can always just go back to the beach and climb into the forest!' Dan called.

'Is that the high-tide mark?' Minnie pointed to where at the base of the cliff there was a distinct colour change from a darker shade of grey to lighter grey above it.

'Yes!'

'We can just climb above that mark and wait for it to go out.'

'Could be hours,' said Dan.

'We could sit on that boulder until the tide reaches the mark and then swim back.'

'Yeah, maybe Minnie. Good thinking! But we

don't know these waters and how the tides are over here.'

Dan took her hand, 'OK. Let's get on the rocks. Up there. We might be able to clamber round.'

He helped her up on to a waist-high boulder from which they could step up to another.

'Is that a cave?' Minnie pointed under the overhang of the limestone cliff at a dark crooked opening.

'Could be, but we are not going in there!'

'But we'd be above the tide, just on that ledge.'

There was a ledge by the opening to what looked like a small sea-worn cave.

They clambered up and were soon on the ledge.

'Hello-eee!' called Minnie as she leaned into the gap.

'What are you doing?'

'Just letting all the snakes know we're here.'

'Snakes?'

'Sea snakes. Yeah. And anything else that's living in there.'

Dan did not look happy. Minnie nudged him with her elbow, encouragingly.

'I'm sorry, Minnie.'

'For?'

'The tide. Amateur mistake. The fog ... I didn't see the tide coming in. It could be an hour or more before we can walk back round.'

'But I thought we were gonna swim back round.'

'That's not a good idea. Look... The currents ... I don't know the currents here... It's too risky.'

Minnie studied Dan's face. He looked devastated.

'This is my second stupid mistake.'

'Dan, it's OK.' She patted his knee. 'What was the first?'

'I let us set off from home, without really knowing how long it would take to paddle over here, and without double-checking the weather report! Your mom would not be impressed.'

'The weather's very changeable here, Dan. Very.'

Minnie wanted to make Dan feel better. She hated to see him beat himself up and he had never before mentioned her mom in that way. As they sat on the rock together, she considered how hard it must be always to be wondering if he was parenting the way the woman he loved would have wanted him to. Every decision he made he must have made with her in mind, not wanting to disappoint her. Even though she was gone, physically gone, Minnie felt her mother's spirit with her always. It was what made her want to explore. She felt safe. She always tried to remember to trust her instincts, as her mother had taught her. She'd said, 'Minnie, think about something carefully, weigh it up, and then if your heart tells you it's the right thing to do, it's likely to be the right thing to do.'

'Dan, we set off yesterday because you knew I wanted to get the quartz here as soon as possible, because I was worried about my Sasquatch friend. You knew that and you did it for me. I'm sorry I put you in a difficult situation.' She gently punched his arm. 'Hey, look, here we are, and we're fine.'

'Thanks. Yeah, I guess we *are* fine.'

'Yeah.'

'Oh no. What if they send a boat while we're in here? They won't see us.'

The water was creeping higher but was not yet at the high-water mark.

'We just have to sit it out. They probably won't try till the fog lifts.'

'Dan, how much battery life have you got on your phone?'

'Less than half, why?'

'Let's explore! There may be another way out!'

Smiling broadly, she held her measuring stick sideways in her mouth to free up her hands and moved to the cave opening.

'Wait!'

Dan hurried after her, turning on the phone's torch. Inside, lit by its white glare, the split in the cliff opened up to reveal a tall, wide cavern.

'Whoah!' Minnie's voice echoed. 'This is big!'

There was a tumble of boulders and loose smaller rocks on the cavern floor, but there was a passage between the boulders that led upwards. Minnie grabbed the top of a boulder and stepped up into the passage.

'Here, wait, I'll go ahead.' Dan squeezed past Minnie and lit the way.

'I can feel a breeze,' said Minnie. 'Which must mean…'

'There's an opening at the other end.'

'Cool.' Minnie's face glowed with the excitement of an unexpected discovery. 'I love caves!'

'Since when?'

'Since now.' They climbed up on to another ledge and Dan shone the torch.

'There.' Minnie pointed at the next obvious point to head for, which was a gaping black arch behind a jumble of loose gravelly rock. They could feel the gentle breeze on their backs, almost as though it was encouraging them onwards.

'How do you feel, Min?'

'Fine. You?'

'I feel OK, which is weird.'

'Why's it weird?'

'Because I'm leading a twelve-year-old girl deeper and deeper into an unexplored cave system.'

'You wanna go back?'

'Let's just see what's through here.'

Dan helped Minnie hoist her leg over the next ledge and pulled her up to standing. The phone's white light showed they were in another cavern, but it was even bigger than the last, much bigger. The roof of the space was as high as a good-size conifer.

Just then the whole space, the cavern and the limestone rock surrounding them, seemed to resound with one single solid *DONK* from somewhere. It was the sound of something heavy, like a boulder, being dropped.

'Was that from above or below us?' Dan asked. Minnie just shook her head.

'Oh, wow!' said Dan. 'What's *that*?'

Minnie grabbed his arm. 'What's what now?'

'Up there! Look! I see light.'

'Don't scare me, Dan. Just speak normally, calmly.'

'What like this?' he asked calmly.

'Yes! Don't suddenly, like, you know ... yell ... please.'

The light, though faint, seemed to emanate from a space beyond where they were, as though it was glowing from above but in the next chamber along.

'Dan, will we be able to find our way back?' Minnie rested against a vast limestone pillar.

'Well, I saw no side passages, no other way to go, except up. Up to here. So, yeah, we could find our way back easily. Don't worry.'

Dan glanced at his phone. 'The battery's almost dead. That's weird. It was at half.'

They climbed on from one rocky ledge to the next, until they stepped into another vast space.

The source of the light was a wide, gaping slot in the roof of the cavern, and Minnie could see vegetation growing over the lip of the opening – bushes and ferns.

'Look, there's...'

Dan's torch died.

'Darn.'

A wide hazy shaft of light cut into the darkness from the mouth of the cave above, lighting the space enough that they didn't need the torch. Their eyes adjusted to the dimness.

Many, many creamy white stalactites hung down from the ceiling, as the same number of stalagmites on the cave floor pointed up to meet them. There was a wide pool of water, with ferns growing around it, which reflected, like a perfect mirror, the multiple twisting conical spikes suspended from above. On one side of the pool the water spilled away over smooth rock, trickling and splashing into the darkness. Shadowy side passages led off from the main cave through wide fissures in the cavern walls.

'Oh...' was all Minnie could say. Tears sparkled in her eyes. Taking Dan's hand, together they feasted their eyes on the magical sight.

'Where does that water come from?' Minnie asked bending down to scoop some up in her hand. She sniffed it.

'A spring. It's seeped through the limestone, from up there.'

'I wish Mom was seeing this.'

Dan squeezed her hand. 'She is.'

Minnie felt the hairs on the back of her neck stand up. At the same instant Dan's hand squeezed hers more tightly.

'Can we get out, up there?'

She pointed to the light source. Dan looked up just as somewhere, quite close by, in one of the black passages, something, or someone, grunted or coughed. It was a short deep deliberate '*humph!*'

Minnie and Dan froze. She whispered, 'What was that?'

'Dunno.'

Dan stepped on to a small boulder, then on to another conveniently positioned larger boulder, and reached his hand down for Minnie.

'Here, quick!'

Something, whatever was in there, *snorted*…

Dan scrabbled easily up on to a ledge, his head was almost out of the gap into the daylight, when, whatever was in there with them *squeaked*...

Minnie was inches behind him on the second boulder, but she slipped, and landed on her side on the cave floor. She glanced at the nearest passage. Something in there moved – she heard breathing, shuffling.

Dan jumped down to the cavern floor. He helped her up. Minnie put the measuring stick in her mouth, so her arms were free, and scrabbled up on to the second boulder. Dan climbed ahead of her so he could lift her and, grabbing both hands, heaved her up and out in a trice.

At that moment, a horrifying, deep, human-like sound shook them from below, somewhere in the cavern. It was louder and deeper than a lion's roar, but sounded bizarrely more like deep rumbling laughter. Minnie and Dan stood staring down into the black crack in the Earth's surface, mesmerised by the bizarre sound. It reverberated deep and long, booming through the system of caves and passages. They could feel it through their feet.

They ran. They ran fast along a game trail from which, through the pines and conifers, they caught glimpses of the fog-shrouded bay.

After running mostly down but occasionally up the winding trail, they emerged breathless above the jagged, pock-marked, grey lump of rock where the quartz still sat, unmoved.

They scrambled down to the beach, which was partially covered by the incoming tide, and sat on the sand, panting heavily. Somewhere in the woods behind them they heard the distinctive hoot of an owl.

'You OK, Minnie?'

She nodded, but she wasn't OK, and neither was Dan. The blood-chilling grunts and snorts, the proximity of whatever it was, the sense of horrifying power that came over them in the beautiful cave, was deeply unsettling. Their hands were shaking.

Dan put his trembling hand on hers. 'Breathe, Min. Breathe deeply...'

After a while Dan pulled her to her feet. Glancing back repeatedly, they walked along the tideline, by piles of washed-up timber, occasional plastic bottles and twisted lengths of seaweed.

'Our mussels are under water!'

The overhang of the jagged rock was now awash, the dark mussels clinging under it no longer visible.

'What are we going to eat, Dan?'

'Seaweed?'

Bending down, he scooped up a length. 'Delicious seaweed soup?'

Minnie was not amused. On top of everything, a pang of hunger gnawed at her stomach.

Where the beach ended, near their canoe, they stopped and looked back up to the far end of the beach, to the bushy, pine-covered grey cliff where the cave was. Minnie still felt slightly dizzy, like she was in a daze, not all there, her thinking slightly muddled. She wanted to sit and be still, to let it all sink in. She walked up the game trail to the shelter like she was sleep walking.

To her surprise, she was suddenly back at the camp. Pulling her sweater off, she flopped down on the blankets. Dan set to hacking off some green boughs with his camp knife. Minnie just stared at the embers of the fire.

'Soon as the fog clears we're raising a smoke signal. They'll be sending somebody to look for us.'

'Will they?'

Dan could see the first sign of worry on Minnie's face.

'They know we are here, Minnie. Connie was expecting us back yesterday. She may even have seen the smoke. So, it's fine. We're fine. We have food and shelter. Well, a banana each, until we can go get more mussels.'

Minnie poked the dwindling fire. 'I know. We're fine.' Dan passed her a banana.

'I had kind of hoped they lived way, way up on this hill somewhere,' said Dan. 'That cave's a little too close for comfort.'

'We don't know if that was them, Dan. That could have been anything.'

'Anything?'

'What's this?' Unnoticed before, between Minnie and the fire, was a shiny green leaf, a big leaf, wrapped around something.

'Dan, look.'

She lifted it. It was weighty. She unwrapped it.

'What the...?' Dan knelt. 'It's a sock-eye salmon!'

'It's huge. As big as a Bigfoot foot!' Minnie laughed.

Dan scratched his head. 'Wow.'

'It was them! They left it!'

'Unless there's some trapper around or...'

'It was them, Dan! Accept it.' Minnie got to her feet and faced the forest, 'Thank you!'

'Thank you!' called Dan. 'Well, I guess I feel much happier about our neighbours now!'

Crouching by the fire, Dan pulled embers over the leaf-wrapped salmon with a stick. He added more twigs and small logs. Minnie knelt beside him to blow on the fire. Flames flared to life, licking at the logs.

Dan glanced around their tree-stump shelter. 'How? How do they do it? There's nothing. No disturbance, nothing.'

Marvelling at the notion that an actual Bigfoot had placed the fish in their camp in the time they were gone, it occurred to Minnie they could still be nearby: maybe they weren't all in the cave. This thought made her stand and peer into the forest – they were surrounded on three sides by an endless parade of seemingly identical conifer trees growing shoulder to shoulder, stretching up and up the steep slope to the summit. Between them was impenetrable underbrush – tall, hardy grass, arching ferns and tangled bushes. Again, the forest was still. She stared into the stupefying quiet.

Somewhere out on the bay, within the fog, the faintest sound interrupted her reverie.

'Dad... did you hear that?'

He'd heard it. Every few seconds a ship's foghorn was sounding a long plaintive *hooo*...

Chapter Ten

'Ahoy there!' yelled Sam. Emerging from the drifting swathes of fog, heading straight towards them on the inflatable rubber dinghy were Sam, Connie and Billy, all waving madly. Minnie and Dan ran down to the beach.

'Hi! Hi!' yelled Minnie, as Dan waded out to meet them. He grabbed the rope, pulling them into the shore.

Dan grinned at the boatload of friendly faces. 'Boy are we glad to see you! We're fine, but...' He trailed off, as Connie grabbed his hand.

He embraced her and Billy together.

'Connie called me, so...' started Sam.

Connie wiped away a tear. 'I saw the smoke yesterday evening! We were so worried.'

'Thank you, Sam!' Dan slapped him on the back. 'Thank you, Connie!'

'My pleasure,' said Sam. 'Happy to make that Alex wait a little longer. He's not happy.'

Connie stepped out of the boat. 'What happened?'

'Holed the canoe on some driftwood!' Dan said as he helped her.

They together heaved the dinghy up the beach.

Sam carried his rifle slung over a shoulder, as he tied the dinghy to a big stump of driftwood. 'How far out was ya when you got holed?'

'Not far, we waded in.'

'Lucky ... real lucky.'

'Gosh. You OK, Minnie?' Connie was holding Minnie's hand tightly.

'Yeah. Had my life jacket on, so...'

'Of course. Excellent,' chimed in Billy.

'We pulled the canoe in and made camp. A pretty cool camp.'

'Wow,' said Billy admiringly. 'You're a hardcore outdoorsy survival expert, Minnie.'

'I know! Wanna see it?'

'Do bears poop in the woods? You bet I do!' And Billy set off in the wrong direction.

'No!' called Minnie. 'It's up there!'

Glancing up at the ridge, there was no smoke from the fire and the redwood stump was barely visible from the beach. Minnie led the way with Connie and Billy close behind her.

They all stopped by the canoe above the tide

line as Sam examined the damaged fibreglass hull.

'Now, you wanna tell me why you came over here?' asked Sam. 'I reckon Connie knows but she ain't sayin'.'

Dan looked at Minnie. She nodded, and as they continued up the trail Dan said, 'Well, Minnie and I had some experiences up in the forest over there a few weeks back. It seems there was a group of Bigfoots living there and they made their presence known.'

Sam stopped walking. 'Did you see one?'

Billy stepped over to Sam, looked him square in the eye and said, 'We saw about ten of them. They ran right past our cabin one night and jumped off the jetty. One of them up close, he waved at us. Yeah, waved. They swam right on over here. How stinking cool is that?'

'Except the one who waved, he didn't swim over,' said Minnie. 'My friend. Rufus. Least, that's what I call him, probably... Not quite decided on his name.'

Dan put an arm around Minnie. 'Minnie saw him go back up into the forest.'

They continued walking up the trail towards

their camp. 'And then those two, Alex and Marshal, got all spooked in the woods...'

'Mighty spooked,' added Billy.

'And took a shot at something...' said Dan.

'And I found blood on a lump of beautiful quartz,' said Minnie. 'Well, I was worried that Rufus was injured and needed help.'

'So we came over here to let his family know,' said Dan.

'Clan,' said Minnie. 'His clan.'

'And how did you intend to do that?' asked Sam.

Billy wagged a finger at Sam. 'That's a very reasonable question.'

'Thank you, Bill.'

'We left that piece of quartz on that big lump of grey rock over there,' said Minnie.

They all paused on the muddy trail and looked over to midway along the beach at the pock-marked grey outcrop with a barely discernable lump of quartz sitting on it.

'That rock's got mussels growing on it,' said Minnie. 'We had mussels for supper last night, Billy-Bug!'

Sam looked at Minnie. 'Why? Why did you leave it there?'

'Oh, because he left it for us to find in the dinghy. With ... with blood on it. His blood.' Minnie explained again.

'Is it still there?' Sam asked, looking over at the rock. 'The quartz?'

'Yes. Look. You can just see it from here.'

Sam scratched his neck with a finger. 'So ... doesn't that mean, they ain't here?'

'Well, this morning I found my baseball cap,' said Dan. 'I lost it in the crossing, blown off my head in the wind. And, somehow, this morning, it was right there, next to the quartz, on that rock! They found it and put it there.'

'Really?'

Minnie detected a note of doubt in Sam's voice.

'Yes, really.'

'That is so cool,' said Billy.

'Maybe a passing fisherman found it?' suggested Sam.

'There were no boats out last night in the storm,' said Dan.

'And no footprints in the sand,' said Minnie. They turned the corner as they reached the fallen redwood and came round the mass of roots.

'And this is our camp,' Minnie announced, as she pushed past the final tall fern on the trail.

'This is great!' said Connie. 'Perfect.' They admired their fallen redwood, hollow-stump home with branches jammed over its roots providing shelter, ferns and moss on the floor, with their sleeping bags and spare clothes hanging within. The fire was smouldering, smoke wafting, and something smelt good.

'We're cooking a fish,' said Dan, bending down to brush the embers off the leaf.

'You caught a fish?' Sam was staggered. 'A big one at that!'

'Well, no,' began Minnie, as Dan grinned proudly at Connie who, along with Billy and Sam, was clearly pretty amazed by their story so far. 'This morning we went for an explore, round on the next beach.'

'That's where we found the footprints by the way,' said Sam. 'Round on the next beach.'

'Right. Well, we didn't notice the tide coming in.'

Dan raised a hand. 'My bad.'

'So we decided to wait on some rocks by the cliff and the tide kept coming up and up, but we found a cave entrance, so we went inside and climbed up into this enormous cavern.'

'You did what?' asked Connie looking at Dan, who was looking pretty sheepish.

'We had the torch on my cellphone so, you know, it was pretty safe.'

'And we found this beautiful cavern, like a glorious cathedral with these... What are they called, Dan?'

'Stalactites and stalagmites.'

'Hanging down. Yeah, and one of them coughed or, like, grunted...'

Sam pulled his cap off. 'One of what?!'

'The Bigfoots,' said Minnie matter-of-factly, 'but I prefer to call them Sasquatches. And then he kinda snorted, to tell us to get out of there. So we did. Through the roof,' she paused. 'It was pretty intense.'

Billy, Connie and Sam were speechless. Dan looked pretty shaken too, as if relating what had happened had somehow made it more real.

Minnie pointed at the fish. 'And then when we got back, there was this *ginormous* salmon all wrapped up in a leaf, waiting for us. 'Cos they knew we'd be hungry.'

'We were,' added Dan.

'Very,' said Minnie.

'We were starving,' said Dan. 'Here.' And he unwrapped the salmon and tested it was ready by breaking off some flesh.

Stunned by their story, the three rescuers sat down where they were, as the fish was passed round. They didn't speak while all of them, including Minnie and Dan, let it sink in. They ate the fish with their fingers.

It was faint, but Dan and Minnie looked at each other when they heard the first wood knock, up in the forest. Minnie glanced at Sam who didn't appear to have noticed it. An answering whistle-warble from closer by made Sam stop eating his piece of fish and look up at Dan.

Minnie, Sam and Dan gazed into the dense forest around their little camp. Minnie suddenly felt like the trees crowding round them were closing in. She felt a presence in the woods, not a dangerous presence but it carried a strong sense, almost an urging, that it was time for them to leave.

She stood up. 'I … I think we should go.'

Yup,' said Dan. 'Let's go.'

He stood quickly, as did Sam, and they started packing up. The blankets, the loose clothes, were stuffed rapidly into their backpacks. Sam and Connie reached up and pulled the green boughs off the roots of the stump, and Billy poured water from a bottle on to the fire. No one spoke.

They hadn't finished all the fish and Billy held it in two hands. 'What should we…?'

Minnie took the half-eaten salmon and placed it on the ground. Dan did a quick check that nothing had been left, and they hurried away, jogging down the trail.

'Keep together,' said Sam. They hurried in single file, Dan bringing up the rear.

No one spoke until they got to the canoe on the beach.

Sam grabbed one end. 'It'll be OK to tow it to the boat; I'll stuff a plastic bag in the hole for now. The *Queen* is just there, look.' The sea fog was parting, showing a pale blue sky and the *Squamish Queen* neat and trim, sitting partially visible, anchored a short way offshore like a ghostly vision.

Sam tied the canoe to the inflatable dinghy, as the others climbed in with the gear. Sam and Dan pushed it out to deeper water so Sam could lower the engine at the back. They climbed in and Sam grabbed the starter rope connected to the engine.

At that moment a very loud crack, like a gun being fired, made them all look back at the forest. A tall, slim pine fell towards them, cracking as its trunk split, smashing on the beach with a *WHUMP!* sending branches, bark and shattered wood spinning through the air.

Billy grabbed his mother's hand. 'Mom…'

'Pull!' yelled Dan, and Sam pulled the starter rope but the engine wouldn't take. A pinecone, thrown from deep in the trees came arcing towards them. It hit Connie on the arm. Sam kept pulling but the engine refused to start.

'Quick!' yelled Dan, as another pinecone flew from the trees and landed with a splash nearby. 'Pull, Sam! Pull!'

Minnie noticed for the first time that just a few trees in from the edge of the ridge, near where the pine had been pushed over, was a giant symmetrical X. Then she saw it – woven in to the shadows, behind a redwood tree but leaning slightly out, was a shoulder, an arm and the head of a very, very large grey Sasquatch. She only caught a fleeting glimpse of it, as Connie flinched when a pinecone splashed nearby, and got in Minnie's line of sight. When Connie moved, a second later, the figure was gone.

With a spluttering growl the motor finally roared to life, and away the boat ploughed through the waves.

With the canoe safely stowed, the inflatable hoisted on to the roof and tied securely, Sam raised the anchor and they set course for Cabin Cove.

Seagulls called in the patches of blue morning sky, circling and wheeling, as the fog dispersed. The boat pitched and rolled gently on the swell, the sound of the engine a deep, soothing hum, easing their passage homeward. Homeward, heading away from what felt to Minnie like someone else's home, to which they'd not been invited.

Billy perked up. 'You OK, Mom?'

Connie smiled at him. 'I'm fine. Thanks.'

Grinning, Dan said, 'You are now officially a member of the B H B A P T B A B... Club.'

'Which is?' asked Connie.

'Been Hit By A Pinecone Thrown By A Bigfoot... Club.'

'That's catchy, Dan,' said Billy.

Sam was in the wheelhouse steering through the thinning trails of mist that shifted in swathes, sometimes making whirls where it met a current of air in the boat's wake. The others, seated on the slatted wooden benches that lined the stern, all stared back at Bigfoot Island.

Connie reached an arm round Minnie's shoulder and kissed her head. Dan patted Minnie's knee and turned to look at her, as she took his hand.

Minnie missed her mother every minute of every day, especially when interesting things happened, like lately. A weariness took over her, and she rested her head on Dan's shoulder. He kissed her curly hair; his eyes filled with tears.

KAAYII

Chapter Nine

Kaayii looked at his mother, Yumiqsu, and she smiled, as did all the Sasquatches gathered in the cavern, when the thought formed in her mind: *father*. The Grey approached his daughter, and they embraced. The Sasquatch clan hummed soft and low and slowly shuffled closer to the reunited pair. Little Yaluqwa clung to the Grey's leg as the others squeezed into one big hairy Sasquatch group hug.

Kaayii and Shumsha climbed out of the gaping hole in the ground to a still-dark, early morning forest. Trees dripped as they walked the game trail winding along the ridge high above the beach.

She stood behind a wide pine. Kaayii stood behind a wider pine nearby. She leant out and pointed through the trees at the fallen redwood – its massive root system stuck up in the air

271

between the trees like the fingers of a hand. Fresh green branches had been cut to lie across the top of the roots, and they could smell the faint odour of smoke lingering on the fibrous bark of the fallen giant.

Creeping closer, Kaayii sensed the humans' energy before he saw them, and knew they were sleeping. Shumsha ducked down a side trail that led to the redwood and, leaping over it, came round the stump from the far side. Kaayii peeped round the ragged roots, and the two nearly seven-foot-tall Sasquatches peered down at the sleeping humans.

They were lying side by side, up the centre of the hollow tree, bizarrely, wrapped in a shiny silver covering. Close enough now to discern the sleeping child's energy, a faint shimmer around her head, Kaayii smiled. Shumsha noticed the shimmer and smiled with him. They looked so vulnerable lying inside the vast dead tree trunk that Kaayii decided to sit and watch over them while they slept – he did not want any of the other Sasquatches to stumble across them. He was sure the rest of the clan would be so tired after all that swimming and climbing up the mountain and swimming back again, that they would slumber on, but he didn't want to risk it.

Shumsha signalled to Kaayii to come with her. She pointed down the trail to the sea. He asked her silently: *why*? And she communicated: *hunger*. He signalled for her to go ahead. She understood that he wanted to stay, and silently slipped through the curtain of concealing trees into the shadows of the forest.

He found a cedar tree close to the ridgeline, overlooking the beach, but hidden off to the side of the trail, with a clear sight of the open stump and the humans lying in it. He sat down amongst the stand of ferns, leaning back against the base of the vast tree, and dozed.

He awakened a while later to dense fog suffused with a low, early-morning light. A squirrel, halted in his climb by the unusual sight of a sleeping Sasquatch, clung to the trunk of a nearby pine, staring over his shoulder at him. Kaayii blinked and the squirrel scurried up the tree to the safety of higher branches.

Kaayii, becoming impatient, crept closer to the vast redwood stump, crouching behind a cedar tree. He could see the two forms still wrapped in their shiny wrappings. He wondered when they would wake up. He threw a stick between the trees, out over the beach. It clattered on the rocks and stones on the shore. The humans didn't stir. He found another stick and flung it further out. It clunked solidly on a sturdy piece of driftwood. The man twisted and shuffled. Kaayii was a pinecone's throw away and reckoned if he grunted the man would hear. He didn't grunt. He waited.

Eventually the man stood, looking at the fog covering the beach and beyond. To Kaayii he seemed worried.

The humans had brought the quartz to the island the previous day, his clan had watched them arrive and had known instinctively that the blood was Kaayii's. They understood that it was a message, and they knew to trust this girl. They had swum over to find Kaayii and to make sure he was well. And now, Kaayii was wondering why the human girl and her father hadn't returned as soon as they had left the quartz. Were they hoping to see the Sasquatches again, like they did that dark night?

Dawn became day and the man collected dry sticks from the nearby conifers and lit the fire. He hoped the rest of his clan wouldn't be drawn by the smell to investigate. Though the forest was too wet for a fire to spread, as it had at their mountain home, he knew the others would be curious. He heard talking. The girl was awake.

From his spot near the cedar he watched them as they walked down the trail to the beach. Stopping by the grey outcrop of rock and looking at the quartz, the girl seemed disappointed. She climbed up on the rock and picked up the man's hat. Kaayii smiled as she performed her happy dance on the rock. The humans hugged and laughed. Now, surely they would leave. But Kaayii was baffled – they didn't go back to their small wobbly boat and paddle away into the fog. Instead, they climbed down the grey rock and walked further away towards the canyon and the cave.

At the end of the beach he lost sight of them as they entered the small canyon where the stone towers stood.

He ran back along the trail towards the cavern, leapt right over the gaping cave entrance near the wooded cliff top and ran on up the path through the cedars and pines, the low scrub and waist-high ferns.

Up on the top of the cliff he could see the girl, who was carrying a thin stick, and the man walking on the beach, just visible through the fog. They were mostly looking down at the sand, searching for something. Kaayii wondered if they were looking for food. If they were, they were looking in the wrong place. He wondered why they didn't pull the mussels off the big grey rock where the quartz was, or eat the anemones in the tide pools, or the sea urchins, limpets, crabs and seaweed.

From his vantage point he noticed how swiftly the tide was coming in. As his father had told him, it swirled around the headland and started to seep into the canyon first, before rushing up the wide expanse of beach where the humans were walking. He wanted to warn them. With his mind he told the man to turn and look back. The man stopped, turned, and looked back to the canyon. Now the humans began to walk back towards him.

Kaayii crept to the edge of the cliff, lay on his belly between two gorse bushes, and looking down he saw that water was already filling the gaps between the tide pools. The humans had left it too late; they'd have to go back and climb up into the forest.

Directly below him they disappeared from sight under the rocky overhang. He thought they must have found a rock to sit on, to wait until the tide went out again. Kaayii was worried, worried they might climb up into the cave, which would not be good, with the big, grumpy grandfather in there, sleeping.

He ran back, away from the canyon. Dropping down in through the jagged opening in the rock, Kaayii found it was quiet down in the cave. Most of the clan seemed to be still asleep in their separate passages, but the Grey and his father were on all fours drinking at the pool of water.

He silently told them to listen, and he looked so worried that they did. Humans were talking, their words echoing up from the caverns below.

Kaayii told them: *hide*. Taashi took the Grey's hand and led him into one of the passages. Kaayii hurried to his mother's passage and crouched low with her and Yaluqwa, who immediately climbed into his lap. They sensed that Kaayii needed them to be silent and they didn't move. He whispered the ancient sound Sasquatches use meaning humans: 'Oomwha'.

They were getting closer. From deep in the

shadows Kaayii could see a light flashing across the top of the cave, lighting up the thousands of cream-coloured spikes hanging there. He looked up at the gaping hole in the cave roof and the small boulder he stood on to pull himself up. The humans wouldn't be able to reach the way out; it would be too high up for them.

He rushed out of the passage, hissing for someone to help. His uncle and father emerged from hiding. Kaayii was trying to shift a tall boulder and only with their assistance did they manage to roll it over. Making a loud, resounding DONK, it fell exactly where he'd wanted it, next to the smaller boulder, directly under the cave opening.

Kaayii hid with the Grey and his father. The humans climbed up and emerged into the main cavern, waving a strong white light around. The light went off, and they stood in silence. It felt very strange to Kaayii to have two humans standing in the Sasquatches' new home. They started talking, and the girl pointed at the gap in the cavern roof.

The Grey suddenly coughed. Kaayii turned to him, looked up into his eyes, and told him: *No. Friends.*

The Grey put his hand on Kaayii's shoulder and with his other enormous hand he covered his mouth and grey, bearded chin.

Kaayii sensed that the sound of something large coughing in the blackness had been enough to terrify the two people. The man stepped up on to the first boulder and took the girl's hand to help her. The Grey could not contain himself. He snorted. His massive shoulders shook. Taashi was holding his hand across the Grey's mouth. The Grey was giggling uncontrollably. His efforts to be quiet resulted in squeaks – high-pitched squeaks like a mouse or a rat might make. This seemed to amuse him even more, and tears rolled down his wrinkled grey face. Taashi had caught the fun-fever now and was grinning broadly as his shoulders shook rhythmically. Through tears they both could see how annoyed Kaayii was, and this amused them even more. Even his uncle Ahniiq had started silently shuddering with a broad grin on his face.

The girl slipped and fell. The Grey stopped giggling. So too did Taashi and Ahniiq. They watched anxiously from the black shadows as the man climbed down to help her up. The humans clambered up the boulders and the man pulled her up. They were just exiting the cavern when the Grey couldn't contain himself and let out a deep sonorous barking laugh that was long and very low, and made all the other Sasquatches, even Kaayii, laugh a deep rumbling laugh along with the old, happy, grey grandfather.

As soon as the humans were out, Kaayii's mother left her hiding place, came in to the other passage and whacked the Grey's arm. She told him: *No! You frightened them!*

Ahniiq looked at the Grey and, smiling, muttered the Sasquatch sound that meant foolish: 'Chump'.

Kaayii hoisted himself up and peered out of the opening. They had gone. He darted away into the woods, wanting to watch over them and to be sure they were leaving.

An owlish *hoot* sounded nearby, and he ran towards it. Shumsha stood in a stand of ferns. He waved when he saw her and she hurriedly beckoned him over. She held two large fish, one in each hand, and nodded towards the humans' shelter. He told her: *yes*, and the young Sasquatches ran directly towards the fallen redwood.

Kaayii stood near the ridge watching the two humans walking back along the beach. They were talking, clearly still tense and fearful, but again they didn't go to their boat. When they passed the canoe and started up the game trail, he signalled to Shumsha, and she knelt to place one of the fish on the ground, wrapped in its big green leaf.

Shumsha ran silently to Kaayii's side and they hid in the bushes behind tall ferns and watched as the humans approached up the trail towards the camp. There were two moss-draped cedar trees near the ridge in a dense stand of ferns, closer to the camp, so they crept round to hide there. The humans found the fish and shouted a happy shout. Kaayii could see they were smiling and was pleased they were no longer frightened. The man lit the fire. Kaayii and Shumsha looked at each other questioningly, both wondering why they weren't eating the fish.

Somewhere in the fog a yearning yowl, like a lonely coyote or a lovesick seal, penetrated the gloom. It came again and again. Leaving the fish in the fire, the man and the girl ran down to the beach. Kaayii didn't understand what they were doing.

A buzzing sound came from somewhere. Kaayii looked around for bees. A small black boat with people in it appeared from the fog. As it drew closer Kaayii could see the small boy, his mother and another man. They all seemed very happy to see the girl and her father standing on the beach. They embraced each other and laughed.

Crouching in their hiding place, Kaayii and Shumsha watched fascinated as the humans talked and laughed. Shumsha asked if the humans were coming to live on the island. Kaayii didn't know. Eventually the group of five humans walked back up the trail to the redwood stump, talked for a while, sat down, and finally fed on the fish.

At that moment a wood knock rang out, from somewhere near the cave. Shumsha grabbed Kaayii's wrist: *Taashi*. He didn't want to alert the humans by knocking a tree so close to them, so Kaayii answered with his whistle-warbling sound, hoping the humans would think the sound was just a bird.

To his surprise the humans began hurriedly gathering their things, apparently getting ready to leave. Moments later Kaayii sensed his father and another presence somewhere nearby.

Standing to search the shadows between the trees, he could see his father and uncle Ahniiq between a pair of conifers. He beckoned them over. Silently running through the pines, past the ferns, and jumping over bushes, within seconds they were beside him.

The two older Sasquatches stared at the human activity on the beach. Ahniiq kept nudging Taashi, pointing at the man holding the killing stick. Kaayii sensed that they were willing the humans to go and were becoming angry. He didn't feel the same way, as he understood humans better than his father. The girl had tried to help him, and she had a special energy, unlike the others.

On the beach, the humans were dragging the black boat into the water and loading their things. They tied the slim canoe to it by a rope and pulled it behind as they all climbed in the boat. Kaayii could see the much, much bigger white boat looming out of the fading fog.

Creaking sounds nearby alerted Kaayii to the Grey who had joined Taashi and Ahniiq. The Grey was rocking a pine tree back and forth and the trunk was beginning to give way. The top branches arced back and forth, bending the slim trunk, until with a wrenching *CRACK* the tree ripped through the neighbouring branches, and fell over the ridge. The top of the tree *CRASHED* on to the foreshore of the beach, sending rocks bouncing, and smashed bits of driftwood spiralling through the air.

The humans froze. Kaayii looked across to his father, but he had moved ... both he and Ahniiq were kneeling by the fire eating fish.

Kaayii was sure the humans were leaving, but the man who brought the boat kept pulling on something again and again. The people kept looking up at the forest, and to Kaayii they looked worried, but the boat just bobbed about on the waves and the man kept pulling. A pinecone flew out of the forest. It hit the boy's mother. Kaayii ran towards the Grey to stop him, but he threw another cone. This one splashed into the water near the boat. The Grey was behind a redwood. Kaayii grabbed the Grey and pulled him back. He told him: *no!*

The small boat growled and spluttered and finally moved off, through the waves.

There was only a thin screen of ferns and grasses shielding the Sasquatches from the beach and the humans hurrying to leave it. Crouched low by the fire, Shumsha handed Kaayii a piece of salmon. The heat from the fire had magically transformed the flesh, and it was the most delicious fish Kaayii had ever tasted.

'Goompoop.'

Shumsha nudged him and pointed up into the forest: *follow me.* So, grabbing another chunk of salmon, he did as instructed and followed her.

Next to the two tall pine trees at the summit of the hill was an even taller tree, its canopy missing, blasted away by a lightning strike. The tree's mottled brown bark had been blackened by fire, and its pale inner bark was visible in the break at the top of the trunk, where the highest branches would have grown.

He climbed it. Kaayii was sure this was the tree he had seen being hit by a bolt of lightning the day he saw the human girl, Minnie, for the first time, from atop his favourite tree over on the mountain.

Sitting in the tall pine, far above the clearing fog, he tried to spot his favourite tree near the summit at High Ridge, but it was too far away. It was all a blanket of green from this distance.

The fog had thinned on the far side and the white boat had stopped moving by the small islands. He could just make out the small black boat, looking about the size of an ant, as it headed to the jetty. Kaayii smiled, and looked across at Shumsha sitting in the other pine. She smiled and looked back at Kaayii.

They walked away from the pines, down through a large open clearing. Shumsha raised an arm and pointed into the forest. On the far edge of the trees the young bull moose was grazing on short green bushes. Kaayii clucked his tongue loudly. The moose looked up. Kaayii waved, and the moose stared a while, then lowered his head and continued grazing.

Kaayii looked across to the high mountain and thought of his friends there. He wondered if Huff and Mook were in the cave, or waiting in the Watcher's Place for him, or ranging far afield across the flanks of the mountain.

Shumsha scooped up some wild onion as they

entered the shade of the forest and handed some to Kaayii. They sat and fed.

Spotting an interesting tree structure, Kaayii pointed at the arched-over slim pine, pinned under another uprooted trunk, with a star pattern of crossed tree limbs constructed over the top of the arch. He asked her: *who made that?*

Shumsha smiled as she placed her flat hand on her chest. From the structure began a grid of straight, stripped trunks all stacked two high, all connected, that continued up the next rise out of sight amongst the firs and cedars there. He grunted his approval. Shumsha nodded at a tree and made a buzzing hum: *bees.*

A short while later, licking their fingers, they lowered themselves from the alder tree, thanking the bees for their honey. This made Kaayii homesick for his forest and as they walked together with their own thoughts, his eyes sought one more glimpse of his mountain home, far off through the trees.

The eleven Sasquatches stood in a circle in the centre of the cavern. Kaayii handed the special lump of quartz to his grandfather, the Grey.

The quartz rested on his vast, black palms. He closed his eyes and wrapped his massive hairy black fingers around the quartz. When he opened his hands the crystal was glowing from within – a shimmering pink light.

Yumiqsu rested her hand on her father's back, Kaayii rested his hand on her back, and so on, until all the Sasquatches were connected. The last in the chain was the youngest, Yaluqwa, who reached up to grasp hold of the longest, lowest-reaching stalactite protruding from the limestone roof of the cavern. They closed their eyes and hummed a song of love for the Grey and for each other. As the hum grew louder the stalactites began to glow a pearly white, lighting the cavern. The vibration from their low hum caused circular rippling wave patterns on the surface of the pool and dancing abstract shadows from reflections in the quivering water.

MINNIE

Chapter Eleven

The rope, thrown up by Sam from the black rubber dinghy, was caught by Marshal. He looped it round the post, just as he'd seen Minnie do four days ago.

'What took you so long?' were the first words out of Alex's mouth. Cristy nudged him. No one answered as they climbed up on to the wooden planks. Sam lifted the backpacks up to them on the jetty.

Minnie and Billy fussed over Musto who wagged his tail wildly, leapt and twisted, and spun round and round, beside himself with joy at seeing them again.

'I see you're all ready to go,' said Sam eyeing the Ashton-Kittos' luggage.

'We've been ready since yesterday morning.'

Alex lifted one of their backpacks as Sam raised

a hand and said, 'Hold ya horses there, fella. We need to debrief.'

'Are you all OK?' asked Cristy.

'We're all fine, Cristy, thank you,' replied Connie as she and Billy and Minnie walked the jetty to the grassy slope. 'Their canoe was damaged so they had to spend the night is all.'

'What damaged it?' asked Alex.

Dan adjusted his cap. 'We hit some driftwood.'

Connie, Billy and Minnie walked towards cabin number one with Musto where Marshal caught up with them. The lanky teenager, glancing back at his father on the jetty, said, 'Hi. Look, I'm sorry about my dad. That thing in the woods really freaked him out. I'm not gonna lie, it shook me up pretty good too.'

'That's OK, Marshal,' said Connie. 'And thank you.'

'He reckons it was a, you know, a Bigfoot, but...'

'Sasquatch,' said Minnie.

'Yeah. After seeing those prints over there on the island, and then what happened up in the woods, I think he feels, like, surrounded somehow, and he just needs to leave. The sooner the better for all of us, to get him away from here, I mean… But … I like it here.'

Connie patted his arm. 'Well you must come back some time.'

Marshal smiled and walked away. He turned back and waved. He crossed paths with Sam and Dan. 'Bye, Dan, thanks for everything.'

'Bye, Marshal. Come back sometime!'

Marshal joined Cristy and Alex waiting by their baggage on the jetty.

Sam and Dan sat on the deck as Sam sipped on a last beer before departure. Sam leaned forward to put his bottle on the table.

'Listen, word gets out about what's been happening here and over there, you could have these cabins booked all year round, with so-called Bigfoot researchers. I don't think that's what ya want, am I right?'

'You're right,' said Minnie, looking at Dan and he nodded in agreement.

Sam continued, 'Now, I ain't gonna tell no one.'

At this double negative Billy raised his eyebrows and glanced at Minnie, who caught his eye and slowly shook her head.

'Can you ask Alex to keep his mouth shut too?' asked Dan.

'I will make sure that fool of a man keeps his mouth shut.'

'They just want to be left alone,' said Minnie.

'Oh, they do,' said Sam. 'They want to distance themselves from humans. Aside from eradicating their forests for farmland, they see us as carriers of disease. We brought influenza, measles, tuberculosis. They've been social distancing for hundreds of years! And who can blame them?'

'So true.' said Connie.

Alex was walking up the slope.

Sam called to him. 'I'll be right there!'

'I, erm … I just wanted to say something.' Alex stood by the bottom steps, scratched his head and looked up at the mountain, then turned and looked over at the island. 'Look, I'm sorry if I've been a jerk. I guess seeing what I saw freaked me out. A lot. To … have them so close… Over there. And … over here!'

'Thanks, Alex,' said Dan. 'Appreciate it.'

Alex passed Dan an envelope, which clearly had a wad of dollars in it. Dan thumbed the cash. 'Oh. Thank you. Paid in full.'

Alex nodded. 'So, what happened on the island?'

'Oh, not much. We made camp, ate mussels, and waited to be rescued.'

'Right, OK, so where do you think that lump of crystal came from? The one I saw in the dinghy yesterday morning. Real early.'

'Oh, *that* crystal. That was a gift from one of them. For Minnie.'

Alex scrutinised them, looking for signs of fun-making. 'A gift?'

'Yeah,' said Minnie.

Alex looked up at the forest. 'How do you know *I* didn't leave it there?'

Dan smiled. 'Er, I asked you, Alex, and you said no. Besides, we know who left it there.'

Alex scratched his head. 'Can I see it?'

'Nope,' said Dan.

Alex shook his head, sensing the conversation was over. 'Anyway, I'm sorry about… But I am anxious to get outta here, Sam, and, with respect guys, we will never return.'

'OK. Good.' said Dan. 'Bon voyage.'

Alex turned to go, then hesitating he turned back.

'You all seem … very relaxed about all this … activity.'

'Oh, we are,' said Billy.

Alex walked slowly away. When he was out of earshot Billy said, '*Not.*'

Alex turned and raised a hand in final farewell, heading up to cabin number four.

Connie stared after Alex as he trotted up the steps and into the cabin. 'What's he doing? He's been cleared out and ready to leave since breakfast.'

A short while later Alex re-appeared.

'All good!' he called, trotting down the steps.

They all stood on the jetty and waved as the *Squamish Queen* chugged away. Cristy and Marshal stood in the stern smiling and waving, while Alex stood in the pilothouse with Sam.

Later that afternoon, Dan had put the canoe on its two-wheel trolley and pushed it up to the standing posts, where he had a stash of tools and paint pots under a small blue tarp. He put the canoe upside down on wooden supports and he applied a fibre-glass patch to the gash in the hull, while Minnie worked in the vegetable garden close by.

'Dad?'

'Minnie.'

'You know Alex said that what he saw was grey? Up in the forest?'

She stopped digging up potatoes and leant on her fork.

'Yeah. Except he said he didn't know what it was.'

'Right. Well, I saw a grey one on the island.'

Dan stopped smoothing resin over the patch and gave Minnie his full attention.

'After the tree was pushed over. Back in the treeline.'

'Grey?'

'Definitely grey. And they are rare.'

'So, you think the grey one swam over from here?'

'Yes, which is good because maybe Rufus was with him,' she said bending down to pick up some spuds, rubbing the earth off with her thumbs and tossing them in the basket.

'Or they came over from the island, after we left the quartz, checked on him, and went back with the grey one. See?'

'All in one night?'

'Yes.'

'OK,' said Dan, clearly unconvinced.

'But I think Rufus was with them. He put the baseball cap on the rock to let us know.'

'Where did he find it?'

'In the sea. Duh!'

'And he left the fish too?'

'Yes.'

'And then pushed a tree over?'

'That was the grey one. Probably when he saw Sam's rifle. They don't like guns.'

'Wow. OK. Good theory, Min.'

'*I* think so.'

And with that Dan went back to work.

'Of course,' Minnie continued. 'We still don't know for sure if Rufus is OK, and whether he is here in the forest or there on the island. I hope he's here.'

Dan looked up from his work and looked at Minnie. 'You know what, Min? I hope so too.'

'You do?' she asked.

'I do.'

Lying in bed that evening, Minnie wondered for the hundredth time what her mother would have made of recent events. She thought about how it had all begun after her mother died and wondered about the timing: whether somehow, by powers beyond her understanding, maybe to do with the energy that connects all living things in this world and perhaps beyond into the past and the future, and into other dimensions, spiralling, looping and passing through each other, somehow her mother had made these events come to be. These thoughts made her weary and she yawned, more than ready for a deep sleep. There was a tap at the door.

'Come in.'

Dan opened the door. He sat on the bed.

'Thanks. Thank you, Minnie.'

'For what?'

'For making my life so interesting.'

She smiled, and gently punched his arm.

'Thank you for taking me and the quartz over to the island.'

'Right.'

'I'm going to make your favourite tomorrow, Dad.'

'Wait. What? Zucchini?'

'Yup. Zucchini and tomato casserole.'

'Thanks, Min. Yum!' He kissed her on the forehead. 'Sleep well.'

KAAYII

Chapter Ten

Kaayii stood in the water, just the top of his massive head above the surface. His wide-set eyes blinked away salty water. The night was perfectly clear and tranquil. The moon cast a silver gleam across the bay, the forest and the sleeping cabins by the softly lapping shore. He kicked and glided through the shallows. As his feet brushed seaweed he reached down, pulling up lengths of kelp, and looping them round his neck. The tide was high so in a few strides they stood dripping on the boulder-strewn beach. Kaayii listened. It seemed quiet, safe, as the two Sasquatches stepped up onto the grassy bank from the shore.

Kaayii turned the handle of the cabin and pushed the door. It swung open. He'd never physically been inside a human structure before and he gazed around, taking in the straight lines, the square angles. There was a big bed and one small bed pushed into a corner. He stood by the door looking around. Next to him was a small square table where he found what he was looking for.

Pulling the cabin door closed, he stepped down off the deck. Quickly and quietly they crossed the open space to the cabin where Minnie and her father slept. Kaayii held Shumsha's hand to increase the energy he wanted to send to the girl, thanking her for helping him. They paused there awhile.

The gate to the garden creaked as he pushed it open. Shumsha waited, watching through the wire fence in the moon shadow cast by the tall pines, sniffing the air laden with odours of rich earth and sap rising in fruiting plants.

Kaayii stood up from where he'd been kneeling and stepped out of the garden to a chorus of wolf howls from high up on the mountain.

MINNIE

Chapter Twelve

The sun was already blazing when Minnie trotted down the steps in the morning, bright and early, her basket in hand. She strolled up the grassy slope to the vegetable garden. Connie was standing on her deck. Minnie waved.

'Morning, Minnie.'

She couldn't see behind the screen of climbing honeysuckle, but Minnie heard the thwacking of Musto's tail on the deck as he perked up at the mention of her name.

She pulled open the squeaking gate to the garden, quickly assessing the high fence to see if any animals had climbed it and bent the chicken wire over. They hadn't. She looked up at her favourite tree and thought about climbing it with Dan's binoculars, to see if she could see the Giant X over on the island.

Kneeling by the zucchini bed, which she had lovingly spread with straw to suppress weeds and to deter snails, she found the peg her mother had placed there, along with all the other pegs in the garden, each with a message on it for Minnie. She pulled it up to read again.

Hi Minnie! This is called Raven Zucchini! See recipe 10 (Dan's favourite!).

Minnie pulled her folding knife from her basket. Under the low, wide green leaves she cut the thick stem of one long, dark green zucchini. She placed it in her basket. Kneeling on the earth, she searched under the leaves to find another. Her hand dislodged something. She lifted it up, and between finger and thumb she held the twisted-willow doll with its straggly moss hair. She gasped. The figure was about as long as her hand.

Only then did she notice that right where she was, in the patch where she had dug up potatoes yesterday, was a fresh footprint, a big one.

'Connie!' she yelled as she flung open the gate. 'Dan!'

She sprinted down the slope.

By the time Minnie returned, breathless, to the

garden with Dan, and her measuring stick, Connie and Billy were standing by the posts.

'What is it, Minnie?'

'Look,' she handed Connie the doll, and as she and Billy examined it Minnie crouched by the footprint. She carefully laid one end of the marked-off stick by the heel, positioning it alongside.

'There!' she declared. 'Seventeen inches exactly! He's back!'

HARBOUR SEAL

GREAT BLUE HERON

LIMPET

BLACK OYSTER CATCHER

SEA URCHIN

SALMON

OYSTER

Bigfoot Fact File

- No one knows for sure if Bigfoot like Kaayii are real or folklore.
- Reported sightings date back to the 1800s. In 1846, stories of the Arkansas Wild Man appeared in newspapers across America.
- The indigenous people of North America have always maintained that Sasquatches, or hairy giants, have shared the forests and mountains with them.
- Every tribe had their own name for Sasquatches in their language.
- Recorded footage, vocalisations, and physical evidence found in forests have been analysed in an attempt to prove or disprove the existence of Sasquatches.
- A DNA report based on fifty samples exists and can be read online.
- The Patterson-Gimlin film footage, from 1967, reportedly shows a Bigfoot encounter and can be watched online.
- Descriptions estimate that adult Sasquatches are around 2.1–3.0 metres (7–10 ft) tall.

Acknowledgements

Penny Thomas and all at Firefly Press, great thanks to you again.

Thanks Jess Mason for your illustrations, such magic from your pen.

Thank you Abi Sparrow and Philippa Perry at SP Agency.

My siblings Richard, Jo and Annabel, my love and thanks to you three.

Thank you Julie Brown, you know what you've done.

And thank you Patrick and Mairi – my dad and my mum.

At Firefly we care very much about the environment and our responsibility to it. Many of our stories, such as this one, involve the natural world, our place in it and what we can all do to help it, and us, survive the challenges of the climate emergency. Go to our website www.fireflypress.co.uk to find more of our great stories that focus on the environment, like *The Territory*, *Aubrey and the Terrible Ladybirds*, *The Song that Sings Us* and *My Name is River*.

As a Wales-based publisher we are also very proud of the beautiful natural places, plants and animals in our country on the western side of Great Britain.

We are always looking at reducing our impact on the environment, including our carbon footprint and the materials we use, and are taking part in UK-wide publishing initiatives to improve this wherever we can.